TIRZAH M.M. HAWKINS

Losing Her

The Monarch's Daughter, Book Two

First published by Tirzah M.M. Hawkins 2024

First edition

This book was professionally typeset on Reedsy.
Find out more at reedsy.com

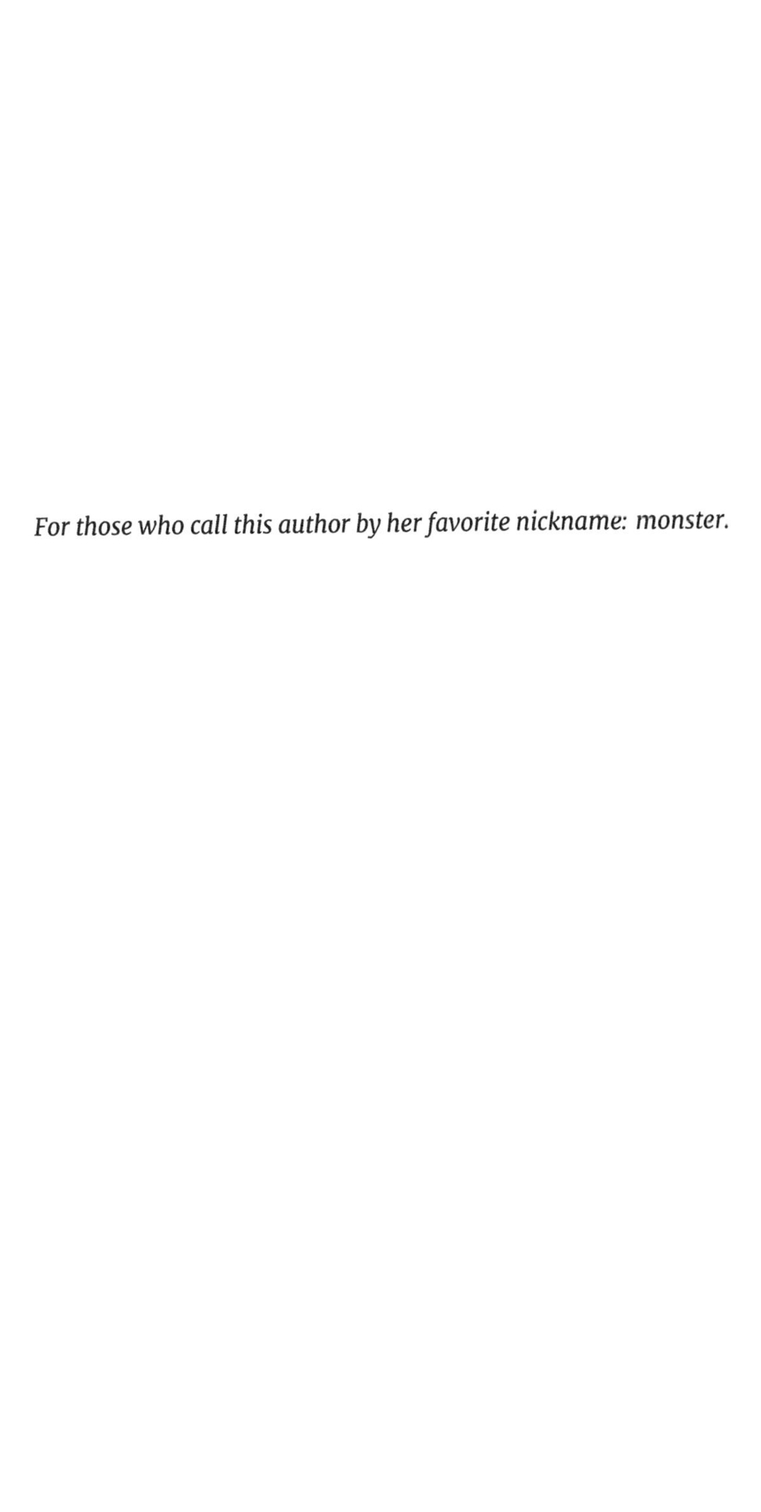

For those who call this author by her favorite nickname: monster.

Contents

1 66: Dead Room (Flynae) 1
2 67: The Pole (Flynae) 5
3 68: The Twins (Flynae) 9
4 69: Concert (Kovad) 13
5 70: Concert (Flynae) 17
6 E71 The Party Starts (Kovad) 23
7 E72 The Party Ends (Kovad) 27
8 E73: The Hornet's Nest (Kovad) 32
9 E74: The Hornet's Nest Part 2 (Kovad) 36
10 E75 Aftercare (Kovad) 40
11 E76 You Saved Me (Flynae) 45
12 E77 Her Room (Flynae) 50
13 E78 Sushi (Flynae) 55
14 E79 Vision (Kovad) 60
15 E80 Vision (Flynae) 66
16 E81 Meltdown (Kovad) 73
17 E82 Evening (Kovad) 80
18 E83 Shower (Kovad) 84
19 E84 The Construct Part 1 (Kovad) 90
20 E85 The Construct, Part 2 (Kovad) 94
21 E86 The Construct, Part 3 (Kovad) 98
22 E87 Collected (Flynae) 103
23 E88 Closet Conversation (Flynae) 108
24 E89 Respect (Flynae) 112

25 E90 Kneel (Flynae) 117
26 E91 I Do (Flynae) 121
27 E92 Fear (Flynae) 125
28 E93 Deal (Flynae) 130
29 E94 Highness (Flynae) 135
30 E95 Use Me (Flynae) 139
31 E96 You (Flynae) 144
32 E97 Planning (Flynae) 148
33 E98 Training (Flynae) 152
34 E99 Healer (Flynae) 157
35 E100 Backward (Flynae) 162
36 E101 Observant (Flynae) 168
37 E102 Spades (Flynae 172
38 E103 Ice Water (Flynae) 177
39 E104 Don't Go (Kovad) 182
40 E105 Nightmares (Flynae) 187
41 E106 Rose (Flynae) 192
42 E107 Xera (Flynae) 197
43 E108 Burden (Flynae) 201
44 E109 Jasna (Flynae) 205
45 E110 Breakfast (Flynae) 210
46 E111 Influence (Flynae) 214
47 E112 Just a Scratch (Kovad) 218
48 E113 Belong (Kovad) 221
49 E114 Ready (Kovad) 225
50 E115 The Slave Mark (Kovad) 229
51 E116 Enough (Kovad) 233
52 E117 Zeresh (Kovad) 238
53 E118 Everything I Want (Kovad) 242
54 E119 I Want You (Kovad) 246
55 E120 Can't (Kovad) 251

56 E121 Losing Her (Kovad) 255
About the Author 259
Also by Tirzah M.M. Hawkins 261

1

66: Dead Room (Flynae)

Flynae wakes up shivering from intense cold. She opens her eyes, closes them, and opens them again. It makes no difference. The space around her is completely dark, offering no light for her to see by.

Tying to sense any nearby energy, she reaches out with hers, but it's like she's in a void. She crawls forward with her hand in front of her trying to find something other than the cold rock she's on.

After just a few forward shuffles, her fingers meet an unyielding surface like a wall. It's more of the same rock that is under her, dead and unresponsive to her touch.

She follows the wall until it joins with another signaling that she's in some sort of room. Then the silence in her mind collides like a punch in her already sore gut.

Kovad?

Nothing.

Kovad?

The darkness presses in becoming a great weight on her chest. Despair pulls her head to the ground until her forehead touches the cold floor. She begins gasping unable to get full breaths.

Kovad! She screams even though she knows he won't answer. The pain in her lungs rivals the ache in her heart at the absence of his voice in her mind. What did Eksar do to him? Images of his body lying cold on the ground flash through her mind. *No.*

Kovad! Tears fall freely from her eyes.

She rolls onto her side, hugging her waist, pressing into the bruise he left there. Could that really be all she has left of him? A bruise. If she squeezed it all the time would she be able to make it never go away?

Kovad, she whimpers while sobs shake her small frame. *I love you.*

It's safe to think those words now. Now that it's too late. She'd known it for a while, since that night he'd left her at the hotel room with his cloak.

Thinking about this makes her miss his smell. He always smelled intoxicating around her because of how much he cared.

Each thought of him being gone makes her cry even harder. She's truly alone for the first time in eight years.

As she struggles for air, she hears his phantom voice of the past telling her to breathe. She feels the essence of his arms around her. All her coping skills had come from him. Each time she needs them, she will remember and mourn him.

She's lying there, no longer actively crying, but still in a ball on the floor when the door opens and light and energy come flooding in. The rest of the room remains like dead matter with the only life she can sense out the door.

A figure stands in the doorway, blocking some of the light and casting a shadow over her.

"Get up." Eksar's voice causes her to recoil in fear.

Flynae stifles the desire to scream and ask, "What did you do to him!" But she won't give him the pleasure of knowing how much he's hurt her by taking Lord Thyde's life. Instead, she struggles to her feet perceiving that she has no choice. He'll just abuse her more if she resists. Her only option is to endure though she wishes her heart would just fail. If only she could die now before she has to miss Lord Thyde for the rest of her life.

Eksar steps to one side as she walks forward. Outside the dead room is a sterile-smelling hallway lit by bright industrial lights. Four men in scrubs stand around a hospital bed equipped with restraints.

Panic grips her throat making it difficult to inhale enough air.

Oh, gods, please, he can't mean to tie me down. The lack of answer twists painfully in her chest. She freezes for a moment before taking a step backward. *I can't do this by myself!*

Flynae wants to be brave and not give Eksar the satisfaction of overpowering her, but it's much harder to endure his presence without Lord Thyde.

"Are we going to do this the difficult way?" His eyes narrow with maniacal glee.

Channeling the last bit of resolve she has, she straightens herself and steps out.

The corners of his lips lift in a sneer. "Lay down." He points to the bed.

Her body begins trembling, overriding her mind's resolve to be strong. She can't bring herself to take another step.

He grabs her by the throat and slams her down on her back. While he keeps her pinned, the men work quickly to secure her. One of them injects something into her neck.

As the world around her fades, she hears an inhuman scream

from nearby.

2

67: The Pole (Flynae)

"What's her status?" Eksar's voice is the first one Flynae hears as she begins to come back to reality. Her body recoils at the sound.

"We've harvested the fetus. It's currently on ice. All we have left is to extract some bone marrow, which we just prepped to do. May we proceed?" There is no audible response.

From nearby, a sharp robotic beep announces her heartbeat.

Fetus? Fennec was right. A cold dread creeps over her, coupled strangely with relief. She didn't have to worry about what Eksar or Seko would have done with a child, but what do they plan to do with the body?

A sharp pain signals a needle puncturing first her hip and then her pelvic bone. Agony radiates from the area. Despite her best efforts to remain quiet, moans escape her.

Flynae opens her eyes and finds Eksar standing over her.

"You're awake. Good. We have more business to take care of today." His eyes are narrow, cold, and impassive; but the smell of his sadistic joy turns her stomach. "Untie her."

The two men in the room move immediately to obey. Soon

she is free from the restraints.

Eksar nods towards the doorway. "Let's go."

The room spins as she sits up. After swinging her legs off the edge of the bed, she has to pause and allow her head to recover from the waning effects of the anesthesia. For a moment, she's uncomfortably aware that she's only wearing a thin hospital gown, but there isn't any room for modesty around Eksar.

"Move now or I will drag you by your hair." His threat issues from him like a growl.

She pushes herself up and clutches the edge of the bed to maintain a vertical position. With great effort, she's able to take slow tentative steps forward. She pauses at the doorway, holding onto it for support.

Eksar huffs at her slow progress.

She advances again as soon as she's able, not wanting him to make good on his words. Every moment brings with it a little more mental clarity and physical stability. After a few more staggering steps, she shuffles unaided down the hallway.

The more she sees of the facility, the more realizes it is not a hospital. It looks more like an insane asylum.

The hallway is lined with doors with round viewing windows in them. She hears beings moaning on the other side. It's difficult to name what could be in there as it sounds neither human nor Kaliah.

A face appears, pressing against the glass to her right, and shrieks. The sound sends her stomach racing into her throat as she flinches back against the opposite wall.

The eyes and ears signal that it is or was a Kaliah. Its eyes are wild. Stringy hair falls over its face. Drool drips from its lips. Whatever they're doing to it has changed it from the regal being it used to be.

Her chest tightens as she wonders if this is what Eksar has in store for her: drive her insane and keep her locked away in a padded room.

The creature growls, snarls, and shrieks. The noises are horrific.

She nearly falls to the floor as Eksar pushes her forward.

"Keep moving."

Flynae uses the wall for another step or two before she regains her feet and can walk on her own.

The corridor continues endlessly. They pass room after room. Behind each door, she senses the presence of more feral things that used to be Kaliahs.

Finally, they reach a door that leads outside. She takes a deep breath of fresh air and closes her eyes to enjoy the feel of the sun on her face.

Eksar grabs her wrist and jerks her forward.

In the middle of the courtyard looms a tall pillar with restraints hanging from it. As he cuffs her into one, the overwhelming smell of dried, putrid blood assaults her senses and causes her stomach to roll.

Gods! What is he doing? She works to not whimper as she braces for what's coming. There is no place in her mind to hide, no one to hold her. She is alone. A tear slips down her cheek.

He locks her second wrist into the shackle and pulls a rope to remove all the slack until she is standing on her tiptoes, her calves and feet straining to take some of the pressure off her wrists.

Please, no. The words come to her mind, but she won't let them pass her lips. It would give him great pleasure if she begged. His scent already indicates that he's enjoying himself.

He rips the hospital gown off her left shoulder. The sound

makes her flinch. Her backside is mostly bare now.

Eksar steps close, so close that his hot breath is on her ear. She recoils from it. His right forearm braces across her back, his right hand at her left shoulder. Something sharp presses against her skin.

When it punctures her, every nerve in her body lights up like it's on fire. She screams. Her body bucks and writhes. He presses against her back harder, keeping her contained between him and the pole.

The agony continues as his hand makes small movements in the skin over her shoulder blade. Each stroke shoots fresh tendrils of torment to her nerves.

Her head grows light and swimmy. Unconsciousness teases her with thoughts of relief while remaining just out of reach. Her body breaks out in a fine layer of sweat.

When he finally steps back a few minutes later, admiring his work, she's panting and dripping sweat. While the nerve pain has stopped, every muscle in her body is weak and shaking from clenching through the anguish.

3

68: The Twins (Flynae)

When Eksar releases Flynae's wrists, her muscles are completely depleted and don't have the strength to hold her up. She slumps to the ground.

With an impatient sigh, he throws her over his shoulder and carries her away from the facility. After a few minutes, he opens a door and enters a building. She sees a wooden floor beneath his feet.

"Father, what are you doing?"

Shame and distress overwhelm Flynae at the sound of her sister's voice. Flynae had done everything she could to hide this part of the abuse from Sekara. If Eksar was done with her, he would have left her cuffed to the pole until she'd recovered. The position she's in leads her to believe that only one thing can be coming next.

"Go to your room." His voice is harsh and stern.

Sekara hesitates a moment before turning and retreating. Flynae hears a door close. She exhales a small breath of relief.

Eksar continues forward and slams a door behind him. He drops Flynae to the floor. The hospital gown hangs off her arm offering her no covering. He pulls it from her.

She retreats inside her mind even though she has little space to go to hide. Her thoughts return to her bedroom at the ranch and the comfort of Lord Thyde's arms around her, bruising her. She remembers the feel of his lips against her ear, his breath on her face, the intoxicating way he smelled.

Her torso clenches in pain as her body trembles and shakes, but she remains in the memory as much as she can for the solace it offers. Tears stream down her face. Moments stretch out and pass like nauseating nightmares.

Eksar gives a final grunt and lifts himself from her.

"That's the first time you've cried," he remarks as he stands up.

She curls herself into a ball and continues to weep. His footsteps begin loud next to her ear and fade as he walks away.

She doesn't move, wishing she could just vanish into the void. Why does she even hang on? Consciousness fades in and out as her body can't deal with any more trauma and forces her to rest.

A blanket flutters and settles over her. A form that mirrors her own lays down and wraps an arm around her.

Sekara sniffs and begins sobbing. "I didn't know," she whispers. "I know that sounds ridiculous now. But I didn't know. I was so self-absorbed. I'm sorry."

Flynae reaches out from under the blanket, finds her sister's hand, and squeezes it. She doesn't have the strength to respond. Sekara cuddles her as she dozes.

A shriek in her ear awakes her with a start. The blanket falls off her body as Eksar drags Sekara from the room by her ankle.

"My daughter does not sleep with trash." His voice is severe with disapproval.

When she is alone again, Flynae forces herself to get up and shower, washing away the scent of Eksar. She returns to her room and stares at the bed for a minute before grabbing a clean blanket and retreating to the floor of her closet. Hiding won't stop Eksar from taking her if he wants her, but the enclosed space feels safer than being out in the open.

"Flynae." A soft voice whispers her name.

She cracks the closet door. Her sister's eyes shine in her direction before Sekara comes in and closes them both in. The twins huddle together.

Sekara begins crying again. "I'm so sorry."

Flynae pets her hair and squeezes her. "Shh. It's okay, dear one. You wouldn't have been able to do anything anyway." She strokes her sister's hair. "Do you know where we are?"

"Moki."

"Where's that?"

"Exactly," Sekara replies a little dramatically.

"Shh. We need to be quiet."

"It's in a completely different sector from Diomede. It's a crushing small planet, too. Each day has only eighteen hours. I hate it. I don't know anyone. Father didn't even enroll me in school." Sekara pauses for a breath and looks at her sister. "And now I'm complaining about me after what he did to you." Her voice breaks down with fresh tears.

Flynae kisses Sekara's cheek and pulls her closer.

"The planet is kind of in this weird lockdown," Sekara whispers. "It can receive communication from the outside, but all outgoing transmissions are completely restricted to the authorities."

Flynae fights off overwhelming dread at these words. She won't be able to communicate with Senice and tell him she's alive. If she's allowed to leave the house in the morning, she'll head to a library and see if there is any news concerning Lord Thyde. If he was reported dead, it would be all over the news.

Kovad? The silence in her head makes her stomach twist and tighten. She just wanted one more word so she knew he was alive.

"What did he do to your shoulder?" Sekara's question interrupts her thoughts.

"I don't know. What does it look like?"

"It says 'E.L."

Flynae shivers. "Eksar Let." *He branded me.*

4

69: Concert (Kovad)

Lord Thyde stands in his place, third in line, waiting for the Emperor to arrive. He can't help but hold his breath in expectation that maybe this time Seko will enter with Flynae on his arm. It's been fifteen months since that night at the ranch, and he's tormented daily wondering where she is and what they're doing to her.

The great doors swing open, and the Emperor walks in alone. Kovad struggles to control his disappointment. He refuses to believe that she'll be forever gone from his life. The silence in his head is maddening. He would give up everything to have the mindlink with her back.

"Something wrong, Lord Thyde?" Seko asks when he's standing in front of Kovad. The Emperor's eyes are narrow and seem to be studying him.

The human knows that his energy gives him away, but he still doesn't desire to acknowledge his despondency. "No, my liege."

"You can't hide your feelings from me. I know what you want. You just might be pleasantly surprised tonight."

Nervous excitement tightens Lord Thyde's chest.

The Emperor flicks his eyebrows upward. "See. Hope." He moves on.

Kovad energetically reaches out beyond the hall and banquet room. If the Emperor truly does know what he pines for, then she has to be nearby. He's about ready to admit that he's being played when he senses her in the area of the building behind the stage. It takes every ounce of discipline he has to remain in his place and not break decorum as a thrill runs through him.

She must know that he's nearby, too. *What are you thinking, Flynae? I want to know.* It's a torment that she is so close yet still out of his reach. And that silence prevails as the only response in his head.

Her energy is stoic with just a hint of nervousness. Her control impresses him.

The Emperor calls for everyone to take their seats. Once he's at the table, Lord Thyde can't take his eyes away from watching the dais expectantly.

Wine is served. The room lights are dimmed while the stage lights up. The orchestra begins playing.

He pays great attention to her energy. It shifts and becomes dignified and regal, reaching a potency that will leave no one in the building unaffected by it. Even he is filled with awe.

Flynae walks onto the stage, disguised as a human, in a revealing glittering deep purple halter dress. The neckline plunges to her navel while the back would be indecent if it were any lower.

Kovad's breath catches at the sight of her. He clenches his fists in his lap to try to keep his composure.

She holds her head high and maintains perfect posture. Her eyes move slowly as she scans the room, but they don't linger anywhere. She meets his only briefly before moving on.

His desire for her burns hot, consuming him. How could she not give him just a little sign of what she was thinking?

Her right-hand moves across her body and grips her left side. He remembers holding her and bruising her waist there the last time they had been together. He has no doubt she's thinking about that moment now. The care and affection he felt towards her then return now.

He watches her inhale and close her eyes for a second. The corners of her lips twitch slightly, almost imperceptibly with a smile. Could she be picking out his scent with so many others in the room? He tightens his fist again, wanting it to be closing over her arm or side.

Flynae breathes again and resets her face and energy as she begins singing. The sound is enchanting and lovely, but he knows she's holding back. She's going through the motions of what's required of her without putting any of herself into it. Every eye in the room is riveted on her.

They don't deserve you, my lady.

She glances at him as if she'd heard him but is quick to look away again.

Dinner service begins, but he is unable to think about food. His entire attention is focused on her. Any drift in his intensity is from thinking about touching her again and hoping that will reignite the link between them.

Flynae finishes a song and creases her forehead in confusion. She turns and looks in the direction she'd come from when she'd stepped on the stage. He watches her eyes widen and her throat tighten. Her jaw clenches as she briefly glares at Seko.

Lord Thyde glances at the Emperor and doesn't miss the smug look on his face. When he looks back at the dais, a young black man with a guitar has joined Flynae. It only takes a moment for Kovad to recognize Will's older brother, Ryen.

The second half of the dinner performance is the two of them singing duets. As soon as the last song finishes, they unceremoniously walk from the stage together.

Couples take to the dance floor while the orchestra continues playing.

Lord Thyde writes a few words on a slip of paper and gives it to the conductor before hurrying backstage.

Across the room, Flynae hugs Ryen. "Now go. You need to get out of here. It's not safe."

"And it is for you?" the boy asks.

"It's nothing you need to worry about, Rye. Please go. While you can."

She doesn't turn as the young man walks away with his guitar case in his hand.

Ryen glimpses Lord Thyde and looks away while quickening his pace slightly.

Flynae bows her head and puts her hand over her eyes with a sigh.

"Flynae."

She spins around, her eyes wide, her breath catching in her throat.

He advances to within a step of her and holds out his hand.

5

70: Concert (Flynae)

The one bright spot in this circus in which she's forced to participate is that Lord Thyde is certain to be there. During her time on Moki, Flynae had gone to the library every day she could get away and watched news videos for hours on end to catch any glimpse of him.

On the first day, she had gone bracing herself for news of his death. Instead, she found footage barely a few hours old showing him with the Emperor. She had run out of the library and the small city they lived near, into the woods, and wept with relief.

She's backstage being prepared when *he* enters the building. She reminds herself to remain focused. Eksar and Seko hadn't broken her so far. She's determined to retain her sanity and dignity for as long as possible.

Flynae feels Lord Thyde energetically searching for her, and a host of butterflies erupt in her middle. Still, she focuses on breathing and remaining calm. It won't do her any good to get worked up before she has to go on stage. They want a show from her. She could make most of them cry if she wanted to, but they don't deserve it. She will show them that she's a member of the royal Kaliah family.

As the lights dim in the audience, she sets her face and shoulders. When the music begins, she walks out onto the stage.

She feels his eyes on her instantly. As she takes in the room, she doesn't allow herself to linger on him. She'd already felt like she'd caused his death once. It was dangerous for Eksar or Seko to know their feelings. If she has any musings about whether or not his sentiments for her have changed, they fade as she picks out his scent.

He wants her more than ever.

Flynae's hand drifts across her torso and touches her waist where he had bruised it. It was an almost absentminded action as it had become a habit whenever she thought of him.

He must have noticed and understood the gesture as his smell intensifies with desire for her. She closes her eyes and enjoys it for a moment. It's the only pleasant smell in a room full of lust and envy.

Flynae works to maintain her stoic composure as she begins singing.

She swears she heard him whisper to her and has to steal a glance. He hasn't looked away.

I want you. she thinks. *I want you to hold me. And whisper in my ear. And never let me go.*

Halfway through the set, the band begins playing a song she doesn't recall was on the list. She knows it, but it's typically performed as a duet. She turns and looks back the way she came and sees Ryen walking up the steps.

How dare they. This was no accident. Ryen was a good singer, but he wouldn't be here if they weren't trying to send her a message. No one she knows is safe.

Flynae struggles to stop herself from trembling as she shoots Seko a glare. The Emperor's face holds a look of satisfaction.

The rest of the performance can't pass quickly enough. As soon as she knows it is over, she hurries from the stage with Ryen. She removes her four-inch heels and throws them across the room in a small fit of rage.

"What are you doing here?" She can't keep the anger out of her voice.

"It's nice to see you, too," he says with a smile. "Where have you been?" His face turns serious. "Will really mis-"

"No, please." She holds up her hand. "I'm so sorry about Will. I really am. But this is not the place." She steps forward and hugs him. "Now go. You need to get out of here. It's not safe."

"And it is for you?"

"It's nothing you need to worry about, Rye. Please go. While you can."

A range of emotions pass across his face. Finally, he settles on acceptance. Ryen picks up his guitar case and walks away.

Her strength and resolve are fading, but she guesses there's still a lot of night ahead. She presses a hand to her forehead wishing it could just be all over.

"Flynae."

There it was, the voice she'd been waiting months to hear. Goosebumps break out from her head to her toes.

Flynae swivels around immediately, her body tense with anticipation.

Lord Thyde walks to her and holds out his hand.

Her eyes dart from his hand back up to his eyes. She struggles to not tremble. Now is not the time to lose it.

"What are you doing?" She checks the doorway, needing to know if they're being watched.

"Asking you for a dance?"

Flynae swallows through a vicious lump in her throat. "Lord Thyde." She squeezes her eyes closed for a moment. "This isn't a good idea. We shouldn't be seen together."

"I don't care." His hand doesn't waver. She can't resist it for much longer.

"What if the mindlink returns?"

"I welcome it. I want you back. I missed you." His voice is filled with an urgent need.

The renewed smell of his affection makes her want to fall into his arms and allow him to hold her.

Because of a memory from years past, Flynae decides to give him one last out. "Are you sure? You were the one researching for a way to end it."

"I didn't know what I was missing out on then. I don't want another day without you with me. Please don't torment me further."

Torment? "Apologies, my lord."

She lifts her hand and places it in his. He grips it tightly. A lightbulb overhead flares and pops. After a breath, she realizes he is there in her mind. *Hi.*

Hi. His response reveals great relief. "May I have the honor of a dance, my lady?"

"It's dangerous." *Though your energy told them more than a dance ever would.*

"I'm willing to risk it if you are."

Flynae nods and gathers her skirt. "Oh, gods." She looks around the room. "I don't know where I threw my shoes."

"Do you need them?"

"No." *I need you.*

He smiles and leads her out to the dance floor. As soon as they enter the room, the music abruptly stops and begins a new song.

Within just a few notes, she recognizes the style. *A tango. Did you plan this?*

Lord Thyde nods. *I told the band to start playing it as soon as I returned.* He begins leading her through steps.

You practiced.

I was hoping I would get the chance to see you again. And I vowed I would dance with you then.

She closes her eyes, her body seamlessly moving in sync with his, and relishes the contact. *How do I know this is real?*

His hand on her waist tightens.

A rush of pleasure runs through her torso.

He digs his fingers in.

You remembered. She sighs.

And I won't ever forget.

I love you. Flynae's eyes fly open and meet his as she realizes what she's done. "Oh, gods. I actually thought that."

His hand renews its grip on her.

Flynae feels the need to explain herself. *I told myself if I ever saw you again, I would tell you.*

His desire to possess and protect her flows from his pores. She breathes it in and relishes it.

Intense pain assaults her nerves. She gasps and barely stifles a scream.

Kovad stops and grips her to him as her body refuses to support itself. *What's wrong? What's happening?*

When the anguish stops, her body still shakes. She regains the ability to stand and steps back from him.

Eksar. One word describes most of the horror in her life. *Thank you for the dance, my lord. It was lovely. I must go now.* She courtesies, and he bows in return.

My lady.

As she walks away, she directs his attention to the mark on her shoulder as a continuation to the answer to his question.

What is it?

A slave mark.

6

E71 The Party Starts (Kovad)

Lord Thyde stands in the middle of the dance floor, feeling her resolve and regal aura, as he watches her walk to where Eksar and the Emperor wait. Flynae doesn't break or cower under their glares.

"Wipe that smug look from your face," Eksar threatens with a harsh whisper.

She turns her head and diverts her gaze but doesn't give in to his intimidation by altering her expression or presence.

"Don't ruin the fun, Eksar. I'll have her in her place by morning." Seko holds out his arm, and she takes it. He flicks his wrist at a nearby servant standing with a stack of envelopes.

Lord Thyde's body shakes with rage. He would rip both Eksar and Seko's throats out with his bare hands if he could.

The Emperor's servant stands an arms-length away now, holding out an invitation. Lord Thyde snatches it and rips it open though he already knows what it is.

The only thing Seko is more fond of than his bimonthly banquets that all his Lords, Admirals, and Generals must attend is his afterparties. These are exclusive to the Lords and occur twice a year on average.

His anger turns to disgust as he realizes the Emperor will bring Flynae. Kovad has done his best to shield her from the depravity of these events. If he had the choice, he wouldn't attend any of them.

At best, they're exotic dance shows. All too often, they turn into orgies of consensual or non-consensual natures. Even though he doesn't partake in any of it, he showers as soon as he can after they're over.

Lord Thyde storms from the banquet hall determined to calm down and check in with Flynae once he's in his shuttle. His throat tightens with bittersweet joy as he realizes again that she's back in his head.

Kovad notices that she's quiet. Her mind is still. He reaches out in a fleeting moment of panic.

Flynae doesn't leave him in agony. *I'm here.* Harem attendants peel her dress and the corresponding tape from her body.

His flight to the Emperor's flagship passes in silence as she's prepared. He's without words of reassurance.

All too soon, he finds himself sitting down with the other Lords, waiting for the Emperor's entrance, fighting to keep his emotions neutral.

It's a large open room with eleven chairs along one wall, facing a stage with three poles. Another quadrant of the room holds two beds while the final corner holds a chaise lounge on a platform.

The doors open. Seko glides into the room and takes the center seat.

Lord Thyde's heart pounds, his stomach in his throat. He feels her approaching and is once more in awe of her overwhelming presence and composure.

Flynae appears, flanked by two Kaliah concubines. She's dressed in a single garment composed of minuscule fabric and metal. The bottom is like a string bikini with decorative chains that run up her bare torso and connect with a bandeau top. Another chain runs from between her breasts to a metal collar around her neck.

Lord Thyde notices the outfit while keeping his eyes above her neck. His hands curl into tight fists at the sight of the collar.

She only glances at him as she's paraded in front of them all to reach her place on the chaise lounge. This seat has always been used to show off the Emperor's candy for the evening.

Lord Thyde doesn't miss how the other Lords ogle her visible skin. He hates that there's nothing he can do to shield her. Everything in him wants to comfort her, but all words that come to mind are empty and useless.

Shh. She meets his eyes with a slight almost scolding raise of her brows.

Kovad realizes she's strategizing, taking in every scent, every wave of energy.

Seko clears his throat, settles back into his plush leather chair, and motions to a servant. The lights over the chairs dim. Music begins.

Half a dozen scantily clad young girls run out onto the stage. It's questionable whether or not any of them are over eighteen. They begin a choreographed dance around the poles and each other.

Drinks are served to the Lords and the Emperor. Lord Thyde refuses. His sight is fixed on the space where the floor and the stage meet, waiting for this to be over.

"Lord Julii." Seko touches the hand of the Lord to his right. "Why don't you get us started this evening?"

Lord Julii runs his hand through his short brown hair, sits forward in his seat, and gives the Emperor a grateful, lecherous grin. He stands and rubs his hands together. His crotch shows a noticeable bulge.

Lord Thyde perceives that many of these details he isn't actually seeing but are coming to him from her vision. She's taking in everything and evaluating it silently. He inhales and smells the room how she does: the stale odor of old sex, candy-smelling perfume on the dancers, the rotten-garbage smell of lust, his torment, and the Emperor's dark, moldy evil.

7

E72 The Party Ends (Kovad)

Lord Julii struts to the stage. The girls eye him warily. Those in the front back up a little. They were clearly not professionals and weren't expecting the interaction; their performance suffers from the distraction.

He steps up onto the stage, grabs the wrist of a blonde, and pulls her into his arms.

She tries to push him away. "No! I'm only here to dance."

"Of course, you are, sugar." He tightens his grip on her, enjoying her struggles. "You're going to dance that pretty little body all over my cock."

"No! Please!" She screams and struggles.

Seko groans. "Would you please shut her up?"

Lord Julii pushes the blonde down to her knees with one hand and holds her there by her hair while he undoes his pants with the other.

Mascara runs down the blonde girl's face in dark rivers. The girls on the stage half-heartedly try to continue through their own tears.

Lord Julii allows his pants to fall to the floor and waves his dick in the girl's face. "How many of these do you think can fit in your body at once?"

"What?" She looks up at him with wide, terrified eyes.

He jerks her hair. "Answer the question."

"I don't know," she wails. "One?"

Nine Lords and the Emperor erupt in laughter.

Lord Thyde feels sick to his stomach. He focuses on his breath but is distracted by Flynae singling out Lord Julii's scent and analyzing it. The lechery coming off the half-naked Lord is a thick, rotting stench reminiscent of a bog.

What are you doing? Kovad had expected her to try to cut off her senses, not heighten them.

Something's off. I'm trying to figure out what.

Of course, something was off. They're both trapped in a room where six young girls are about to be gang-raped by nine men for the Emperor's pleasure, and there wasn't a damn thing he could do about it. After that, who knows what the Emperor has in mind for Flynae.

Seko turns to Lord Thyde with a wan smile. "I do wish you could learn to loosen up and enjoy the show, Lord Thyde." He furrows his forehead with care. "It would bring me great joy."

A desire to relax washes over Lord Thdye briefly. When it passes, he's left with an even greater feeling of disgust.

There! she exclaims.

Kovad risks a glance in her direction. Her bright green eyes stare back at him.

Did you feel that? Her heart races with excitement.

Feel what? His pulse quickens to match hers.

The blonde begins gagging and choking as Lord Julii pushes himself completely into her mouth.

Lord Thyde rubs his forehead with a damp palm.

He pushed you. Flynae's attention returns to the man forcefully jerking the blonde's head back and forth. She digs deeper into his energy.

Who? What? Lord Thyde works to clear his mind and understand. *Can you explain what you're talking about?*

Flynae stifles a gasp. *They're all enchanted.*

Enchanted?

That's the human word for the control Kaliah can have over them. Seko is making them do this.

Then what makes me different?

You aren't. She turns back to him. *You just don't watch porn. Or have a secret desire to hurt women. He uses you as an assassin and interrogator, not a rapist.*

Lord Thyde thinks about all the times he's acted as Emperor Seko's executioner. There are several murders he's committed that he isn't proud of and feels guilty about. *Am I still enchanted?*

No. Not by him anymore.

When did that happen?

The moment you touched me for the first time. Remember how confused you were?

He recalls feeling like he was waking from a dream as he had walked away from her that day eleven years ago.

Her eyes move over the other Lords in the room. *Seko is pushing them to fulfill their darkest fantasies. The ones they would never admit to their wives or families.*

Lord Julii bucks his hips a final time and groans. He releases the blonde's hair. She falls to her hands, coughing up bile and semen onto the floor.

Lord Julii turns halfway around. "All right. Who's going to help me educate this little slut? Show her what her body's really for?"

Lord Elika and Lord Norgan jump to their feet, circling the girl on the floor, and begin undressing.

"No! Please!" Her cries echo shrilly in the enclosed space. "Leave me alone! Please! I want to go home!"

The other girls huddle together at the back of the stage now, holding each other and crying. Their performance has been forgotten for something much more interesting.

The Lords standing around the blonde pick her up by three of her limbs and carry her over to a bed while she continues to beg and scream.

I know how to stop this.

You do? He feels the shiver that runs through her body.

Brace yourself. She begins wrapping a protective layer of energy around him. *You're going to want this.* She closes her eyes.

The blonde shrieks in pain.

Flynae jumps.

She begins listening to the girl's screams and brings to mind every painful memory she has one after the other: Lord Thyde cutting her father down, Eksar raping her for the first time, running away from Will, being given to the Emperor, awaking alone in the dead room thinking Lord Thyde was dead, injections that made her scream, shrieks of tortured Kaliah. One after another she brings in all the pain she can find until she's visibly trembling.

What are you doing, Flynae? he thinks softly so as not to distract her.

A tear slips from her eye and runs down her cheek. Then another. They begin streaming down her face.

The room quiets until the only sounds are the sniffles and cries of the blonde. Everyone pauses. One by one, every human in the room except for Lord Thyde begins bawling. The Lords surrounding the blonde wrap her in a blanket and step away holding their heads in their hands.

Flynae opens her eyes. Her throat and chest tighten.

Emperor Seko glowers at her with glowing crimson eyes. He stands up and walks over to her.

She doesn't flinch, doesn't blink.

Seko slaps her hard across her face almost knocking her off the lounge.

Flynae turns her head back to glare at him.

With visible rage, he roars in her face, grabs the chain connected to the collar, and jerks her to her feet. As he pulls her from the room, he calls out, "With me, Lord Thyde."

Oh, gods. I'm sorry.

Why are you apologizing to me? Kovad follows them down the hallway with great trepidation.

I didn't want to involve you. I was the one who kicked the hornet's nest.

8

E73: The Hornet's Nest (Kovad)

Lord Thyde alternates between watching her long, crimson hair swish back and forth as she walks or looking at her silent bare feet as she takes each step down the metal corridor. His body is a knot of tension wondering what the Emperor is going to do while she barely exudes any emotion.

Two of the Emperor's Kaliah guards fall into step behind him.

Flynae keeps her head up and her shoulders back as much as she can with Seko yanking on the collar around her neck.

Lord Thyde recognizes with horror the hallway they turn down. It leads to the interrogation chambers.

When they enter one of the rooms, Seko directs his guards to secure her to the cuffs hanging from the ceiling in the middle. He pulls the energy disguising her as a human while unlocking the collar around her throat and stripping her body bare.

"You've had your fun." His face is so close to her as he talks that she feels his breath hot on her cheek. "Now, let's see how you like mine." He pulls her hair forward over her shoulder.

Lord Thyde finds himself staring with dread at the perfect marble skin of her back.

Seko walks to a wall that holds a myriad of whips, chains, canes, and other torture utensils, selects a whip, and places it in Lord Thyde's hand.

Kovad stares down at it while his mind refuses to acknowledge what he's holding. As soon as he recognizes it, he drops it. "No."

Seko gives him a sly grin and lifts his eyebrows in glee. "Oh, but you will, my Lord Thyde." The Emperor draws a knife out of a pocket as he walks back to Flynae. Starting at her hip, he traces it up her side.

"I know you have a thing for this girl," he continues, "and she has greatly displeased me. You are both going to suffer for it."

Lord Thyde shakes his head. "I won't do it."

"Suit yourself." Seko runs the knife along her cheek. "If you refuse," he drags the knife up to the tip of her slender ear, "then I will remove her ear by slicing off an inch of it at a time until all that is left is a gaping hole in the side of her head."

Flynae's body visibly tenses.

Lord Thyde's breath catches in his throat. His heart pounds, and his palms start sweating. He considers begging but knows it will lead to nothing. There is no way out of this nightmare.

Seko knicks the top of her ear.

Kovad. Please. The waver in her thoughts reveals her trepidation while she continues to keep her body mostly still.

I can't flog you. He groans aloud in anguish.

The Emperor makes another cut.

Kovad. Please! I'm sorry I got you into this.

This isn't your fault. None of this is your fault. His hand trembles as he leans down and picks up the coil of leather off the floor.

Seko's eyes narrow while his grin widens. He steps aside, giving space, and waiting to see what Kovad will do.

Lord Thyde coils the whip around multiple times, getting a feel for it like he always does before a flogging. Swallowing is difficult. Breathing comes with great effort.

"I know what you can do," Seko voices a warning. "And I'll know if you hold back."

It's okay, she whispers.

He shakes his head. *This is not....* He can't finish the thought.

He takes a step and brings the leather down across her back leaving an instant angry red welt where it touched her. In slow motion, he watches her body rock forward from the impact. The chains above her rattle. The heels of her feet lift off the ground. She releases a hiss of air. His rage and disgust build.

Seko moves his head from side to side while making a tsk sound three times. "I warned you." He steps up to Flynae and puts an arm around her waist while maintaining eye contact with Lord Thyde. "This is what happens when you don't give me your full effort."

The Emperor lifts the knife to Flynae's cheek and draws a shallow cut across it. He steps back and waves his hand in a "continue" motion. "Let's try that again."

Kovad presses the knuckles of his free hand to his forehead while squeezing his eyes shut. He can't do it again.

She appears in his mind, her head high, but her eyes are begging. *It's okay. You can do this. For me.*

He strikes her again, this time with his full force behind the motion. All the air in her lungs exits in a gasp. Her body rocks forward again. She loses her footing and hangs by her wrists.

Lord Thyde watches her feet as one by one she gets them back underneath her and stands upright again.

With an anguished cry, he turns and flings the whip across the room.

Emperor Seko chuckles.

9

E74: The Hornet's Nest Part 2 (Kovad)

"I've never seen you so distraught, Lord Thyde." The Emperor takes a deep breath and exhales with clear annoyance. "Pick up the whip," he growls.

"No." Kovad shakes his head and sets his shoulders.

Flynae approaches him in their shared mental space, takes his hand, and looks up into his face. Overcome with the desire to protect her, he wraps her in his arms.

I know it's a lot to ask, she says softly.

"You think you have a choice right now?" The annoyance in the Emperor's voice is apparent. He grabs a butane lighter off a shelf and walks back to Flynae. "Actually, you do have a choice right now, Lord Thyde." He begins heating the blade of the knife. "You have the choice to decide what she looks like at the end of the night. A few marks that won't even leave a scar or permanent disfigurement." He brings the hot knife up against the top of her ear and begins cutting.

Kovad, please. Her entire body tenses. One of her heels lifts from the floor as she squirms.

"I'll do it." He forces his voice to come out level and calm.

Seko pauses and evaluates him. He lowers the knife and steps away with an expectant look.

Lord Thyde turns and collects the whip.

Thank you. Flynae relaxes against him in their space.

His vision blurs with rage. She's expressing gratitude for a flogging. He raises his arm and strikes her again. She lets out the tiniest whimper as her body pitches forward as much as the restraints will allow. The Emperor closes his eyes briefly in pleasure.

Seko gives the motion for another. And another. The marks begin to ooze blood where they crisscross.

The Emperor holds up his hand. Lord Thyde knows it is too soon to feel any relief.

Seko takes her by the waist and turns her around. The motion twists and shortens the restraints forcing her onto her toes. She keeps her eyes tightly closed not wanting to have the image of him holding a whip forever burned into her memory.

I can't look. She sounds apologetic.

No. Don't look at me right now. He doesn't want to see himself through her.

Seko pulls her hair to the side revealing the rest of her naked body. "Show me some of that great precision you have, Lord Thyde." He draws a diagonal line across the top of one of her breasts. "Lay one right here."

After a resigned sigh, Kovad lands a perfectly placed mark where the Emperor indicated.

Seko traces the opposite side. "And a matching one here."

The second lash is a mirror image of the first.

The Emperor allows her to twist back around. "Continue."

After a handful more strikes, she tries to get her feet back under her and can't. She hangs from her wrists. Blood trickles down her legs.

Kovad's resolve weakens.

Seko motions.

He lifts his arm and adds another stripe to her back.

She barely twitches.

"One more," Seko whispers.

Lord Thyde raises his hand and brings the whip down hard, knowing that if he doesn't deliver it won't be the last.

The Emperor moves to Lord Thyde and takes the whip from his hand. "Don't ever disobey me again or I will not be so lenient next time."

He tosses the whip to a guard, returns to Flynae, and lifts her chin. Her eyelids flutter halfway open. "I wanted you to be awake for this." Seko undoes his pants and drops them to the floor.

Lord Thyde stands frozen in horror.

Inside his mind, she takes his hands and turns him away. *Don't look. Be here with me. Sit down.*

Something solid touches the back of his legs, and he sits. She steps between his legs and rests on his knee.

Seko grunts, and Flynae's body whimpers.

When Kovad turns his head to look, she reaches up and stops him, holding his face in her hands in their shared mental space.

Her thumb gently caresses his cheek. *I missed you.* She leans her forehead against his.

When the chains rattle in the background, she brings to mind a violin playing to drown out the noise.

I missed you. He holds her tightly, his ire rising as her form shakes.

Minutes painfully drag on like hours. Maybe three pass before Seko groans in orgasm. He drops her legs and walks to the door not caring that he's naked from the waist down.

Lord Thyde stares at the blood and semen dripping down her legs, unable to look away. Her body dangles from her raw, bloody wrists; her chin rests on her breastbone.

Seko pauses before exiting. "Since you're so infatuated with her, you can clean her up. I'll send for her when I want her back."

10

E75 Aftercare (Kovad)

Lord Thyde removes his shirt. Tears blur his vision as he releases Flynae's wrists. He wraps the garment around her torso, lays her head over his shoulder, and holds her there with one arm around her upper thighs.

Her hand reaches up and curls around his neck. Her thumb caresses behind his ear causing shivers to run through him. He's reminded how much he's missed her.

Rage and anguish simmer beneath the surface as carries her out into an empty hallway and barks orders into his comm. "I need a medic bay prepared for a flogging and rape victim." The word rape almost sticks in his throat, and he watches with horror again as the Emperor drops his pants and approaches her hanging body.

Memories flash through her mind bringing him back to her: bright overhead lights, injections that burn beneath her skin, fighting against bed restraints, twisted Kaliah faces.

No. No. No. She begins trembling.

No, what? He presses his face against hers, his free hand gripping her arm since he can't embrace her without causing her more pain. *What is frightening you?*

No medical facility. Flynae's breath quickens. She begins weakly pushing away from him as her flight response erases rationality.

Okay. Relax. Please don't fight me. He strokes her hair and holds the back of her head until she begins to calm again. *We won't go there.* He opens the transmission again. "Disregard. Bring everything you need to my quarters. And get someone on a consultation with Dr. Lamb at The Albatross Hospital on Diomede."

"Yes, my lord," is the reply.

The corridors seem like an endless maze as he hurries to the hangar. His flagship, The Destroyer, is on standby just a short shuttle trip away. No amount of distance is enough to put between her and the Emperor, but getting her off the same ship is a start.

Flynae fades in and out of consciousness. Each time she comes to, she releases a weak gasp of pain right next to his ear and renews her frail grip on his neck. Every sound of agony from her increases his ire and misery. He tightens his free hand into a fist, wanting to rage, but he chokes it back for her. There will be time for that later.

They're landing on The Destroyer when one of his medics gets back to him. "Lord Thyde, we spoke with the manager of the Albatross. They said that Dr. Lamb retired, and they don't have any contact information for him."

Kovad suppresses a surge of rage and frustration. He's going to have to contact Senice to find out where to get kya leaf to give her for pain.

Sorrel. Flynae's thought is so quiet and random that he doesn't know if she's delirious or aware.

What did you say, baby? He strokes the back of her head.

He didn't retire. He was due for–. Her mind fails. For a moment, she can't find the words to get her point across. *Changed name. Dr. Sorrel.*

Kovad speaks into his comm. "Call the Albatross again. Speak to Dr. Sorrel. Get whatever he advises here NOW." *Thank you.*

Her thumb flutters against his neck causing a rush through his body. The pleasure brings more anger knowing that his hand had been the one to cause her so much pain. When he hears the haunting sound of the whip striking her flesh, he pushes it from his mind and focuses on caring for her now.

The hallways pass by in a blur as he hurries while trying not to jostle her. When he reaches his room, he pauses to take a breath. The medical staff are waiting for them in the hall and follow him inside.

Her hand grips him weakly when she smells other people.

It's okay. They're here to help. I need to set you down now.

Her hand stiffens, and she begins trembling again.

I won't leave you. He squeezes the back of her head.

The image of her hanging by her wrists, naked and bloody, appears in his mind bringing tears to his eyes. One of the medics behind him sniffs. He realizes Flynae's crying.

He turns on the humans waiting to assist as they all start sobbing. One by one they cover their faces with their hands unable to deal with their most painful memories in the presence of Kaliah tears. Through gritted teeth, he says, "Wait in the hallway until I send for you." *Incompetent,* he groans to himself though he knows it's not true. Without the knowledge acquired through the mindlink, he wouldn't have been any more capable.

They bob their heads and make a hasty retreat while wiping their eyes and trying to get themselves under control.

You can cry. It's all right. Lord Thyde caresses her hair and holds her as best he can without hurting her further. He waits patiently not wanting to rush her until she regains her composure. *I need to set you down. I will be right here holding your hand.*

She nods, resigned to trust him, though she doesn't fully understand what is happening as she barely clings to consciousness.

Sleep, my lady. I'll be here when you wake up.

That's enough for her to relax and slip into a disturbed unawareness. She cries out when he lays her down, but she doesn't fully come to.

He speaks into his com and calls the medics back in. The lead doctor tells him that the medication Dr. Sorrel had indicated was still a few hours away.

"You will keep that on hand from now on," Lord Thyde says.

The doctor nods in response.

Lord Thyde sits by her head holding her hand while they clean and dress her wounds. He tries to keep the entire nightmare of an evening from replaying in his mind during the process. Flynae moans whenever he lingers too long in the memory.

Hours later, her wounds are dressed, she's been given a sedative and pain reliever as approved by Dr. Sorrel, and the medics leave. Exhaustion overtakes him. He falls asleep with his head near hers, holding her hand.

Images of Seko's leering face plague his slumber. He hears the whip impact her skin and watches her body lurch. The Emperor drops his pants.

Flynae cries out in terror and pain.

When he lifts his head, he sees her trying to push herself up in an alarmed frenzy. "Wait. It was a dream. Calm down. Please." His last few words come out as a plea when he sees the fresh red blooms on the bandages on her back from her effort.

She lies still and takes a moment to recall where she is as her heart slows its fevered pace. *Kovad?*

I'm here.

Would you hold me?

He hesitates, evaluating the painful process that will take. "Are you sure?" She's naked on the bed except for the bandages on her back and the sheet lying over her.

She nods. *Please. I need to feel you against me.*

"Okay. You're going to have to help hold the sheet. I don't know how else to do this."

He wraps the covering around her and makes sure she has a grip on it before lifting and pulling her onto his lap. She suppresses her wail of pain from the movement as best she can. When he has her settled and close, she reaches up until her fingers find his skin above the collar of his shirt. Her fingertips rest there as she fades back to sleep.

11

E76 You Saved Me (Flynae)

Flynae smells him as she comes to before she even opens her eyes. She inhales deeply of his intoxicating scent and brings her face close to nuzzle his neck. It's been so long since she's been able to drink his aroma in, and she relishes it now. Her fingers run up from the skin at his throat to the back of his neck and into his hair. A thrill runs through her torso as his scent changes at her touch becoming needy and possessive.

Kovad grabs her arm, opens his eyes, and looks into hers. Through his vision, she sees her wounds have healed overnight. His sight blurs with tears. Knowing that it's safe to hold her, he grips her body tightly and presses his face against hers. She lets out a gasp as the air leaves her lungs in a rush, pushing away her panic at being restrained.

Once again, he sees the whip fall across her back leaving an oozing welt. He watches her regain her footing over and over while he marvels at her strength and willpower. The memories of the night before overwhelm him, and tears spill down his face. He presses his forehead against hers and silently sobs, his body shaking with emotion.

For the last fifteen months, he hadn't even known if she was alive or what awful things might be happening to her. The first day that he gets her back turned into a nightmare beyond his imagining.

"Lord Thyde," Flynae whispers. *Kovad.* "Thank you." *Thank you for being so brave for me.* Her fingers grip his scalp and pull his head even closer.

I beat you. His hand squeezes her side tightly and jealously. Her body responds with another rush of pleasure at the pressure and his smell.

You saved me. She runs her fingers through his hair. He shivers and grips her even harder. Pain has never felt so blissful.

He begins to calm down and opens his eyes to find her scarlet hair filling his vision. "I want to kiss your head."

"Are you asking?" Her breathing is shallow with desire.

No. Because I don't know if I can stop there. I'd want to kiss my way down to your neck. He can't hide his deepest thoughts from her. His hand traces a path down her ear and across her nape.

Her skin burns beneath his touch before desire turns to panic. She can't get enough air and pushes away, clutching the sheet around her naked body, and moves from his lap to the edge of the bed. Her hair falls like curtains shielding the sides of her lowered head. She hides her burning face with her hands, overwhelmed by his lust to possess and claim her.

Within a moment he's on his knee in front of her reaching to hold one of her hands. "Flynae, I'm sorry. I would never do anything without your consent."

She gives up one of her hands to be enveloped by him. "I know." *I'm damaged and used. Why do you want me?*

"You are the most amazing thing ever. You are everything to me. *MY* Monarch. *MY* Empress."

His declaration is startling and unexpected. She uncovers her face and stares at him for several moments without response, while her heart nervously gallops inside her chest.

Needing to unfreeze them both from this moment, she moves their hands in a small up-and-down movement. "Okay. This is all overwhelming right now. Can we just start with some clothes and maybe some food?"

"Yes, of course." Kovad kisses her fingers before releasing her and jumping to his feet. From his closet, he retrieves one of his shirts for her to wear. He turns around while she stands up and slips it over her head.

She brings the collar to her nose and inhales. "These really are my favorite *dresses,*" she says with a smile. "They smell so good." *Though I don't often go commando.* Without provocation, her body begins visibly shaking.

He pulls her close into his embrace as he examines her mind for the cause. Her breathing is steady. Her mind is clear, but her body trembles uncontrollably.

How can I help you? His eyes squeeze shut in a grimace.

I don't know. Not much helps. Her cheeks flush with embarrassment at her lack of control.

What do you usually do?

I sit in a dark closet until it passes.

Lord Thyde's rage sparks again before he can bring it under wraps. "Maybe you just need distracted." He leads her out to his office barely letting her body inches away from his as they walk, sits down at his workstation, and pulls her onto his lap. "What do you want to eat?"

Flynae relaxes against him. "Fish sounds good."

He pulls up a sushi menu on the computer screen. "What do you want?"

She recoils having found another source of overwhelm with all the choices.

Lord Thyde begins selecting one of each option of sushi and nigiri. "What kind of sake do you like?"

"I've never had it."

He adds five different varieties to his order.

She looks up at him, her eyes drinking in every bit of his skin along his neck, jaw, and cheek. "Who are you expecting to eat all this?"

"I'm just providing you with options." He grips her side while finalizing the order and sending it.

Flynae stifles a moan as she hopes he leaves a bruise.

He sighs. *I don't want to hurt you.*

Your bruises don't hurt.

In his mind, he hears a younger her scream. Traumatic visions of the past flash through her mind so briefly that he doesn't recognize much except for his footsteps and Eksars's face.

"What was that?" He squeezes her.

"What?" She's not lying, but he knows she's denying whatever he just heard.

"What just happened?" He closes his eyes and goes into their space.

She's standing guard in front of a door. From the other side, a child version of her is screaming. When he advances she stands firm, shaking her head.

What are you doing, Flynae? Let me help. The cries continue causing him deep anguish. The door rattles and shakes.

She stands her ground. *I can't. Everything I can't handle is on the other side of that door.*

Let me handle it with you.

I can't. If it's let out–. And I'm cut off from you again–. I can't deal with it on my own. The shaking in her body intensifies. She shakes her head in refusal.

"Let's try another distraction." Kovad rubs her arm.

His voice in her ear brings her back to her body. She's drawn her knees up making herself small. Her feet rest on his other leg. She pulls the shirt down as she lowers her legs to the floor.

"I have something I want to show you."

Flynae inhales his excitement and braces to be overwhelmed further.

12

E77 Her Room (Flynae)

Kovad takes her hand and leads her to the door. A tug on his arm stops him as she pauses before he can open it.

"Where are we going?" Flynae looks down at herself. "I'm not really embarrassed to be seen in just your shirt, but I'm still feeling half-naked."

"Just across the hall. The only people we'll pass are the two guards outside my door. And if they so much as glance at you, they'll find themselves missing their eyes and begging on the street before the day is over."

Her eyes widen with horror. "Lord Thyde. Please don't do that. You know it's almost impossible for a human to not look at a Kaliah."

His face softens, and he squeezes her hand. "Okay. I won't be harsh on them, my lady."

You called me baby last night. Her stomach flutters at the memory.

I did. I didn't think you would remember.

A smile tugs at the corner of her lips at his assumption that being only half aware would impact her memory. Her free hand fidgets with the hem of the shirt. *Was it an accident?*

It was more instinct than accident.

Does that mean it might happen again? Her chest tightens in anticipation and longing for a specific answer.

Would you like that?

Her cheeks burn while he looks at her in a way that says she's the most beautiful thing ever. *I would.*

Then I wouldn't think of disappointing you. "Come." He gently pulls her. They walk out into the corridor together.

When she comes into view, the guards do glance at her. She feels their eyes move down her body and legs before snapping back to the wall before them. To her relief, he notices her observation but doesn't react.

Just across the hall and ten feet to the left is another door. He stops before it and brings her in front of him.

"Close your eyes," he whispers though part of him wished he could take the liberty of putting his hand over her face.

"You're making me nervous," she says while obeying. "You are," she inhales and dissects his aroma, "one step away from giddy, my lord."

"I've been waiting a long time to show you this." Kovad's body presses against her as he leans forward to turn on the light. He holds her upper arms and walks her forward a few steps. "Okay. Open."

Her jaw drops as she gasps, taken entirely unaware. "What is all this?"

Every inch of the walls, ceiling, and floor before her was painted to look like a forest. Above her is a canopy of trees with hints of blue sky shining through. The walls are colored with tree trunks and shade flowers. Beneath her feet, the floor is a carpet of painted petals.

A couple of feet in front of her sits a plush couch in front of a deep cherry wood coffee table. Over the back of the sofa is a soft, fleece blanket. The other side of the room holds a baby grand piano.

"Do you like it?" he whispers.

"It's lovely, but I feel like I'm missing something. I don't understand."

"If I ever had the pleasure of having you aboard my ship again, I wanted you to have a space of your own."

Her chest heaves as she struggles to take deep breaths. "You made me a room?"

"Maybe slightly more than a room." He takes her hand and leads her to a door on the left, but pauses before opening it. "Are you alright? Do you need a minute?"

"There's more?" Her throat tightens making breathing and swallowing difficult.

He nods, his eyes narrow with concern.

She takes a deep breath. "I'm ready."

Beyond the other side of the door, the forest painting continues. In this room are a queen-sized bed and a dresser with a matching vanity and desk.

Lord Thyde releases her to walk over, open a drawer, and pull out a pair of dance shorts in the brand and style she usually wears.

Flynae shakes her head in surprise and disbelief as she takes them from him. "Thank you."

He turns around to allow her to slip them on.

A scene from the previous evening plays in her head from his viewpoint of her hanging naked by her wrists. What was the point of her being modest now when he'd seen every inch of her body just hours ago?

For a moment, the air around her is too hot. Her shame and embarrassment overwhelm and threaten to suffocate her. Even the too-big neckline of his t-shirt feels restricting.

With an effort, she pushes the feelings inside the compartment she's created for them. Briefly, the child trapped within cries before it's cut off.

Lord Thyde stares at her as her face and demeanor adjust to nearly perfect neutral. A strong feeling in his gut tells him that what she's doing is likely to have unforeseen consequences. There is no hiding the fact that he doesn't like it.

Unwilling to have a conversation about it, she dismisses his concern and turns to the door across from the one they entered. "What's behind that one?"

"Your shower." Kovad struggles to keep his voice even as every cell in his body wants to break down the construct she's created in her mind.

When she looks at the final door, flurries ensue within Flynae's core. Whatever is behind this one has meaning for him. His controlled excitement wanes as her nervousness builds.

She sighs and collects herself again. "You don't have to feel bad." After another inhale, she adds, "Or worried." Her hands twist together in front of her. "Maybe you could just...." Her head drops. *Hold my hand?*

He holds his hand out, and she steps forward to take it.

"I didn't intend to overwhelm you." His voice is soft and gentle.

"I know. I also know that whatever is behind this door is significant. You paid for all the rest of this to be done. Whatever is behind there was one hundred percent you."

"That's true."

"You're very delighted with it and are doing a great job of not even giving me a glimpse of what it is."

A slight smile appears on his lips.

"So maybe call it stage fright?" Flynae shrugs. "I can't imagine that I wouldn't be thrilled..." *But I'm not handling strong emotions well right now.*

"We can wait."

She shakes her head and steps towards the door. "No. I can do this. Just be close." She grips his hand, and Kovad moves close behind her.

With a press of a button, the door retracts into the wall and overhead lights come on.

Flynae's mouth falls open. "What did you do?"

13

E78 Sushi (Flynae)

The room is a spacious walk-in closet. Hanging from the racks on three walls are almost a hundred different dresses in a wide array of styles and colors.

Flynae leans back into him and rests her head on his chest. "You picked out all of these?"

Kovad wraps his arms around her shoulders and touches his chin to the top of her head. "I did."

After a moment of enjoying his embrace, she steps forward into the middle of the room and turns around. The whole thing is a little incredulous to her.

"You made a shrine for me, Lord Thyde," she says with a giggle. It's a musical sound that fills him with joy.

"That laugh alone was worth it."

With her eyes closed, she examines the feel of the entire space. "You also spent close to three hundred and twenty hours in here." She looks at him with wide eyes and a straight, serious face. "About an hour a day after it was completed?"

"Roughly."

"Did you miss me that much?"

Kovad walks to her, and she allows him to pull her into his embrace. "Every day without you was torment. I didn't know if you were alive or dead. If you were alive, I didn't know what was happening to you. I couldn't be there for you." One of his hands slides down her back and grips her waist tightly causing a thrill to run through her.

Everything within her wants to tell him to squeeze her harder. The brief thought alone was enough for him to comply with her desire. She can't quite stifle a moan. The low noise makes him tighten his grip again.

The comm on his wrist beeps.

"The food is here."

She whines before stuffing the emotion away and collecting herself. The air is thick with his concern. She takes a few steps back out of his arms.

He sighs. "My thoughts were that we would eat and then do some training together if you're up for it."

"Yes. Entirely. I don't have a lifesword though."

"How long will it take you to make one?"

Flynae follows him as he walks to the dresser and opens a drawer. Inside are a dozen cherry branches similar in size and shape to the one she had used to make her first lifesword as well as a small chisel set to carve with.

She selects one to examine more closely. "Less than two hours," she says with amazement at his foresight. "Is there something you didn't think of for me?"

"If you find something, I hope you'll share it with me."

Her face and ears burn.

"Come." He takes her hand and leads her back to his room.

The box the sushi arrived in is enormous. He had selected nearly one of everything on the menu.

"I'm not sure my desk is big enough for this."

"We could just spread a blanket out on the floor."

Within a moment, he strides to his room, returns with the comforter from his bed, and spreads it out on the floor. She sits cross-legged, grateful that she has shorts to wear now, and begins pulling out the mini platters of food.

He stands there admiring her still in his shirt until she pauses and looks up at him with her large, bright green feline eyes.

"Are you going to join me?"

"Yes. It's been quite a while since I've had a picnic. And I kind of got lost watching you."

Her cheeks turn an endearing shade of red. "I need a drink." She reaches into the box and lifts out one of the sake bottles. "I'm hoping this has alcohol in it."

He laughs as he sits down across from her. "Yes. It's rice wine."

She pulls one of the bottles out of an insulated sleeve. "That one's warm." The next one is wrapped with an ice pack. "And that one's cold." Her face lights up. "These little cups are adorable. Asian pear sounds yummy."

Lord Thyde can't help but stare mesmerized, watching her delight in discovering something new.

Flynae brings a hand up over her eyes like she's shielding them from the sun. "Okay. Blink or something. You're going to make me blush again. Do you want hot, cold, or room temperature sake first?"

He takes a deep breath. "Whatever you want, my lady."

She selects one at random, fills the provided thimbles, and hands him one. He takes a sip while she tastes hers and then drains her cup. The alcohol has a slight bite that finishes in a soothing warmth.

"Was that impolite?" She realizes she'd treated the drink like a shot.

"Not at all. I got it for you. Have as much as you want."

She pours herself another glass. By the time he finishes his, she has the first bottle mostly gone and is opening the next.

After several sushi rolls, many pieces of salmon, and three bottles of sake, she stretches out on her side on the blanket with a contented sigh. "That was lovely. Thank you."

"You're welcome." He struggles to keep a sudden rush of rage contained. *I would do this with you every day if I could.*

A lump forms in her throat. *I know.* She packs the extensive amount of unfinished food back into the box while leaving the remaining sake out.

"How do you feel about me sitting on this while I make my lifesword?" She pats the blanket beneath her.

"If that will be comfortable for you then absolutely. I'll get some of my computer work done while you're doing that." He moves over to his desk.

Flynae drags the blanket over close to him. "Would you take off your boots and socks?"

Kovad raises his eyebrows. "Why?" he asks as he bends down to comply.

"Because I want to put some of both of us in my lifesword. And it's easier if we're touching." She sits down and crosses her bare ankles against his. "Yours isn't inscribed is it?"

"No." He holds up the plain piece of metal that he wears on his belt.

"Would you like me to inscribe it?"

"To what purpose?"

"The runes give it extra potency."

"Then I would be honored." He holds his lifesword out to

her.

"Show me where you hold it."

He ignites it to get an accurate feel of his hand placement.

"And when you hold it with both hands?"

He stands up to keep the grip natural.

"Got it." She reaches out, and he gives the hilt to her. "Would you like it enchanted as well?"

"Excuse me?" It's his turn to revisit the evening before and recall what the other Lords were willing to do because of enchantments.

"Yes, it's the same concept. But this makes the lifesword its own conductor or generator of energy. It's no longer coming from you."

"By all means. You may do to mine whatever you are doing to yours."

14

E79 Vision (Kovad)

Lord Thyde struggles to focus on the work in front of him while Flynae sits at his feet, carving their hilts and speaking elven words softly. He finds himself noticing the skin of her ankles against his or listening to her melodic voice chanting mystical words. Every movement she makes causes her hair to shimmer like a river of crimson that catches his eye. He fights the desire to just sit and watch her while wondering if he has a say in the matter. She mesmerizes him with her grace and beauty. He would be content to watch her every moment for the rest of his life.

His thoughts must have distracted her. Flynae glances up, meets his gaze, and gives him a smile that makes his heart ache before returning her full attention to her project.

He forces himself to return to checking reports, but the screen before him blurs.

The energy around and between them grows and swirls, caressing them and binding them together. When she sets down her hilt and picks up his, the energy swells. The lights overhead flicker, and his computer beeps as it reboots.

The sense of space between them diminishes. She no longer feels like a separate being, but an extension of him. Their energy combines to pour into his lifesword. He's powerless to look away. Time stops as they breathe and their hearts beat in perfect synchronicity.

"Alright. The first part is done." Flynae says.

Kovad blinks and finds himself slightly out of breath as his eyes refocus on her.

"The next part might get a little intense." She squirms and repositions as if trying to get comfortable again.

"Because that wasn't?"

"Comparably? Probably not."

He takes a deep breath, readying himself for the completely unknown.

She watches him while suppressing a grin as she waits for him to ready himself.

Kovad can feel the thrill running through her body and knows that she's barely keeping her emotions at bay as well.

She tilts her head a little. "Are you ready?"

He shakes his head. "As ready as I'll ever be."

She closes her eyes and begins to recall the memory of being four and enchanting her first lifesword with her father. As a little girl, she sits on Issiah's lap as he instructs her.

"Now we bring them close to our hearts," Issiah says softly in her ear. "And then we lay back and allow the energy to work. Don't force it. Don't resist, Flynae. Melt into it."

Flynae takes both hilts and holds them between her breasts. She places her feet on top of Lord Thyde's and lays back on the blanket. She listens to her father's voice as he begins chanting and whispers the elven words along with him.

The energy in the room heightens and flows through every

inch of their bodies, caressing like a lover.

He watches her arch her back in pleasure and feels a surge of desire for her rush through him. He closes his eyes hoping that will help him control the growing arousal flooding his being.

Relax, she whispers to him.

After a breath in response to her suggestion, Kovad opens his eyes and finds himself someplace else.

The room is bright and spacious. A fresh, soft breeze flows through the open French doors. Before him is a canopy bed with nearly sheer silks hanging from the sides.

He pulls back a panel of the soft fabric to find Flynae napping peacefully on the bed. She's wearing a long emerald green gown. Thin spaghetti straps leave the marble skin of her upper chest and shoulders uncovered. He drinks in the view, feeling his need for her growing.

She opens her eyes and smiles as he lays down next to her.

"Hi." She reaches up and caresses his cheek.

His skin burns deliciously under her touch. "Hi."

"You seem to have come up here with a purpose."

He brushes a strand of her hair back from her face. "I need you."

"Mmm. And what do I get out of it?"

"You get anything you want, Flynae."

"Anything?" The corners of her lips turn up in a playful smile.

"Anything. Everything. All I can give you."

She trembles in anticipation. *Hold me. Bruise me.*

He runs his hand across her body and grips her waist tightly. When she moans under his touch, his pants become uncomfortably tight.

"That's not everything, Kovad. Don't hold back on me." Her

chest swells and ebbs with her breath.

He tightens his grip.

"That's it." She runs her fingers through his hair and pulls him down to kiss her.

Her lips part slightly for him, and he dives his tongue into her mouth. The sweet, intoxicating taste of her increases the ache in his groin. He moves to kiss her neck.

"I love you, Kovad."

"I love you so much, baby," he whispers into her ear.

She shivers.

He renews the pressure on her waist, pressing his thumb into the sensitive middle of the bruise, the place that centers her the most.

"I want to feel your skin against mine." She tugs at his shirt, fumbling to get him free of it.

He refuses to help, relishing her growing desire for him.

When only his arms are left holding the shirt between them does he move his hand and toss the shirt away.

While he has the use of both his upper limbs, he stands and removes the rest of his clothes before returning to reclaim her mouth and side. His attention drifts between his desire to ravish her body and being sure his hold on her is tight enough to keep her anchored in the moment.

"May I remove your dress?" He won't progress further without her express permission.

"As long as you hurry back to me." She tenses, bracing herself for the brief distance.

He pulls the straps from her shoulders and down her body revealing every inch of her. He hesitates briefly taking in the only view he wants to see for the rest of his life. Her side already shows a slight purple bruise where his hand has been.

She opens her legs for him, and he lays between her thighs. His lips find hers again.

Flynae runs her fingers down his back making his whole body tingle.

He renews his hold on her side. *Are you okay? Are you ready?*

Yes, my love.

Be here. With me. He slips inside her and relishes at her gasp of delight. He keeps his movements slow and controlled, intent on making love and being in the moment with her. Every sound she breathes makes him crave her more.

She inhales the sweet scent of his desire and passion for her. *You smell delicious.*

You taste delicious. His free hand runs along her torso, brushing the side of her breast, making her shiver. *I've wanted you for so long.*

You have me—every day. I'm yours. She arches her back, allowing him deeper.

He slides his arms beneath her to grasp her from both sides. Her exhale of pleasure makes him even harder.

The sound of her orgasm is enough to bring him to climax. He remains inside her while their bodies relax and come down. He keeps his grip tight on her side and kisses his way up her ear.

"Lord Thyde." Flynae's voice, barely audible, calls to him from outside the room.

Something taps the top of his foot.

"Lord Thyde."

He doesn't want to leave her and the bed they're sharing, but the image is fading.

Kovad opens his eyes and finds himself back in his quarters on The Destroyer with Flynae sitting on a blanket at his feet.

The first thing that strikes him is how much younger she looks. The image of her in his dream or vision looked at least five or six years older than she is now. The face he sees through her eyes is five or six years older than the one he wore in her vision. How did she age while he grew younger?

"What was that?" he asks.

While Flynae's eyes are wide and her breathing is heavy, her demeanor is calm, her emotions tucked safely away. "A possible future."

"It's only a possibility?" The thought of the vision or dream not happening is terrifying to him.

"The future is never certain. Especially one so far away." With a trembling hand, she holds out the metal hilt for him. "The lifeswords are finished."

15

E80 Vision (Flynae)

Flynae focuses on the lifeswords while she works, aware of Kovad's attention on her, but determined to pay it no mind. It helps that she wants to relive the memories to remember the words to say. Her father's voice speaks calmly to her from the past as she listens to him tell her how to empower the weapons.

Lord Thyde's sweet-smelling scent and intense gaze on her bring her partially out of the past. She glances up and sees his face transfixed by her. The corners of her lips involuntarily lift. His heart responds by slightly increasing its beat.

She returns to her work.

Once she's finished with her lifesword, she sets it down and picks up his. The energy around and between them intensifies to an overwhelming level, and she struggles to breathe normally. The room lights blink. The computer restarts to avoid frying by the surge.

The distance between her and Lord Thyde diminishes as their energy becomes one and his lifesword soaks it up. She's aware of being the sole focus of his awareness.

After an hour of struggling to exist and function in the suffocating yet blissful energy, she sighs and looks up.

"Alright. The first part is done."

Kovad's eyelids flutter repeatedly like someone coming out of a trance.

"The next part might get a little intense." She's preparing herself as much as she's warning him.

"Because that wasn't?"

If she was slightly less overcome and fearful of the intimacy of the situation, she would have laughed. Instead, she swallows the lump in her throat and pushes her emotions down deep. She knows she'll have to pay for ignoring them later, but they're too much now.

"Comparably? Probably not."

Flynae watches him breathe and squirm briefly. The unfamiliar and his inability to have any control of the situation are uncomfortable to him. She doesn't let her smile show. It could be misconstrued as unkind instead of just being a symptom of her discomfort and nervousness. Her body hums with energy. Not just hers, but their combined energy, and it's exhilarating.

"Are you ready?"

Lord Thyde moves his head back and forth. "As ready as I'll ever be."

She closes her eyes and steps back into her four-year-old self. She's sitting on her father's lap as he teaches her how to craft her first lifesword.

"Now we bring them close to our hearts." Issiah's voice is soothing and pleasant. "And then we lay back and allow the energy to work. Don't force it. Don't resist, Flynae. Melt into it."

She picks up the hilts, holds them over her breastbone, and

lays back. Issiah's words flow through the past and out of her mouth. The energy they bring tingles within and around her body like the touch of a lover. Her spine arches in pleasure, and the smell of Lord Thyde's desire for her heightens the sensation. She senses the tension his arousal creates in him.

Relax, she whispers to him.

Suddenly, she finds herself elsewhere lying on a comfortably firm mattress. A soft, warm breeze blows across her bare arms and shoulders. She inhales and recognizes the scent of her favorite planet: Halaa.

Lord Thyde's steps approach, coming up a nearby staircase. They echo of urgent necessity. As he approaches the bed, she inhales the seductive scent of his passion for her.

She looks at him with a grin as he lies down beside her.

"Hi." Her hand desires and finds the skin of his cheek. She relishes the feel of the heat her touch causes in him.

"Hi." He studies her. She knows he's examining her state of mind and emotions so that he doesn't overstep her boundaries.

"You seem to have come up here with a purpose." She relaxes further as he sweeps her hair back from her face.

"I need you." His words are like a breathy growl that makes her body sing.

"Mmm. And what do I get out of it?"

"You get anything you want, Flynae."

"Anything?" A playful smile forms on her face.

"Anything. Everything. All I can give you."

Her body shivers. The excitement running through every inch of her threatens to overwhelm her. *Hold me. Bruise me.* Her side throbs with a necessity only he can fulfill.

Kovad's hand slides with a gentle caress across her body and grabs her waist. The pressure makes her moan, but it isn't quite enough to satisfy her.

"That's not everything, Kovad," she whispers between breaths. "Don't hold back on me."

His hand constricts and presses deeper.

"That's it." She rewards him by reaching up, stroking her hand across his scalp, and pulling him down to her mouth. When she parts her lips, he thrusts his tongue inside, tasting her, before moving on to her neck.

"I love you, Kovad."

"I love you so much, baby," he whispers into her ear.

When she trembles in response, his thumb presses into the bruise he's created. The pain is grounding and reminds her to be with him. Here. Now.

"I want to feel your skin against mine." She grabs the middle of his shirt and pulls until she can find the hem. First, she tries lifting the front, but that doesn't get her anywhere.

He smiles as he watches her struggle but doesn't offer any assistance.

Flynae moves her hands around to his back and tugs at it from there. Finally, she has it mostly inside out and halfway off. Only when she's gotten his head free, does he remove his arm to release it completely from his body.

While his hands are otherwise unoccupied, he gets up and removes the rest of his clothing. The lack of contact threatens to bring terror. It's a brief eternity before his body is against hers again. His lips crash into hers. His hand grips her side, fiercely at first, but the pressure is enough to keep her from slipping out of the present. She notices his attention drift back and forth between his delight in touching her, kissing her, and what she is thinking and feeling.

Flynae relaxes under the gentle weight of Kovad's torso over hers. Still unsure of her role during intimate moments, she returns his kiss and caresses his arms and shoulders.

"May I remove your dress?" His voice sends a thrill of euphoria through her and deepens the aching need for him that excites and scares her. The questions are important. He never moves faster than she's ready for. He never takes what she doesn't give.

"As long as you hurry back to me." This is the last hurdle, the last lack of contact and pressure from his hand.

He starts at her shoulders, pulling the straps of the dress off her, and continues down until she's completely bare. For just a moment, he relishes the sight of her body that she's freely giving to him.

After only a few seconds, she can't take space between them. She opens her legs, and he accepts the invitation to lay between them. Finally, his hand is on her side again, his lips back on hers.

Are you okay? Are you ready?

Flynae inhales. His care and concern overpower every other emotion he's feeling right now. She knows that he wants her to feel safe. *Yes, my love.*

Be here. With me.

When Kovad slips inside her, she gasps in pleasure.

With great control, he moves his hips slowly against hers.

As her ecstasy builds, her breath becomes more shallow, like a pant.

His scent changes as her sounds contribute to his desire for her. She takes a moment to slowly inhale.

You smell delicious.

You taste delicious.

She trembles as he traces a path down her torso with his free hand, brushing the curve of her breast.

I've wanted you for so long. He digs his fingers into her side until she gasps again.

You have me. Every day. I'm yours. She arches her back, deepening the angle of him inside her.

His arms encircle her, gripping both sides of her now. When she moans from the blissful pain, his cock hardens.

The pressure inside and outside is enough to tip her over into a trembling, full-body orgasm. He finishes with her.

With a start, Flynae finds herself back on the floor of his room on his ship. The lifeswords buzz against her torso. Between her legs aches and throbs. The emotions of want and desire threaten to overpower her. She chokes on them, her eyes threatening tears, before she can push them down and lock them away.

She sits up and sees that he's still in the vision. She feels his body humming with pleasure.

"Lord Thyde." Her voice is barely above a whisper. It almost feels heartless to wake him up and bring him back to this world. But the knowing that he's still inside her in the vision is too much to handle. Her hands shake. Breaths come with great difficulty.

"Lord Thyde." She pulls her feet away, cutting off the physical contact now that he's beginning to awaken.

His brow creases with confusion when his eyes land on her face. They had both noticed the aging variations within the vision.

"What was that?"

She takes a deep breath. "A possible future."

"It's only a possibility?" His smell changes from aroused to fearful. She senses his trepidation at knowing he might not ever have what he just experienced.

"The future is never certain. Especially one so far away." Her hand shakes uncontrollably as she extends his hilt out for him. His attention to her trembling makes her face and ears hot. "The lifeswords are finished."

16

E81 Meltdown (Kovad)

Lord Thyde barely notices his lifesword in her hand as he watches Flynae's arm shake. He sees her tense her jaw in a desperate effort to get her body under control, but the trembling only worsens with her efforts.

Her cheeks redden, but she doesn't blink nor withdraw her arm.

Wanting to end her embarrassment, he takes the weapon. The hilt pulses and hums in his hand like a living entity.

"What did you do it?" He looks at her, his eyes wide with awe. *I don't think you'll ever cease to amaze me.*

Flynae draws up her knees in front of her body and hugs them, which makes her look so small. Kovad wants to scoop her up and hold her.

Something in her pulses at the edge of his ability to detect. After inspecting it, his best guess is that it's a tidal wave of emotions she's dammed away. The defenses against them are beginning to weaken. If she doesn't allow herself to feel them soon, he worries they will completely overwhelm her. They'll most likely do that anyway though.

After a deep breath, she responds in an even voice. "The lifesword is its own power source now. It won't get dim even if you are exhausted. It may have other surprises for you. Lifeswords connect with their owners in different ways. There is no way of knowing in advance what those may be." She covers her mouth as she stifles a yawn. He's aware of exhaustion settling into her.

Lord Thyde examines the runes she's etched in it. Each crevice glows with a soft, golden light.

"How do I activate it?"

"Don't push your energy at it like you're used to. Think of it like-," she glances around the room searching for the right words. "Like a light switch. But a mental one. Just flick it on." She grabs her hilt and stands up. With just the slightest thought directed toward it, her lifesword ignites with a fiery crimson blade of light.

Lord Thyde notes the subtle energy she used and replicates it. His weapon responds by creating a glowing blue blade. The hilt no longer feels like something separate from him but an extension of his arm.

She responds to his thought. "It will be much more difficult for it to fall or be knocked from your hand." She holds out her arm, palm down, and opens her fingers. Her lifesword clings to her like a magnet.

You are magical, Flynae.

Her cheeks blossom crimson. "You can do it with yours too." She nods, gesturing for him to try.

Kovad holds out his hand and finds that his lifesword holds to him of its own accord. "Only because of you."

She shrugs, dismissing his wonder because of her discomfort. "It's just how Kaliah make lifeswords."

"No." His voice comes out a little sternly to get his point across. He wants her to be proud of what she accomplished. "We both know that you just performed elven magic." He remembers her obsession with elves and how she feels less than because of the difference in their features. He doesn't want her to belittle what she's just done.

Flynae's eyes don't waver from his, but she doesn't respond in any way. Her mind is silent; her emotions locked away.

When he perceives she has no response, he says, "Shall we go try them out?"

She tenses. He doesn't know why, and he doesn't like that. Whatever she's constructed in her mind acts as a barrier between them.

She glances down at what she's wearing. *Can I get dressed first?*

Of course. Please tell me what you need or want.

She hesitates. He senses her fear before she's able to hide it away. He discovers she doesn't want to leave the room without him. The corridors and strangers in them scare her.

Lord Thyde stands and offers her his hand. "May I escort you, my lady?"

Flynae accepts and grips him tightly. *Thank you.*

He feels her rapidly disintegrating. The facade she's trying to maintain is crumbling. Her body visibly shakes. Each moment of seeing her like this is agonizing to him, but he must keep his calm. He won't let his emotions contribute to her inner struggle.

Kovad leads her across the hall and waits for her in the first room. He tries to keep a mental distance as she enters the walk-in closet to give her privacy to change. For a distraction, he observes all the little details of the forest painting he's spent hours staring at while thinking about her.

Oh, gods, he hears her swear. From her eyes, he sees the green spaghetti-strap dress from the vision. *You picked out and bought that dress.*

Before he even has time to respond, she's pushed down her emotions. He doesn't have time to fully understand what she's feeling.

Lord Thyde withdraws again as she pulls his shirt over her head. A few moments later, she walks out, her cheeks slightly aglow, in a long, pink strapless gown. Around her waist is a deep purple belt from which her lifesword hangs.

For a moment, all he wants is to take in her beauty. Then she blushes and tenses beneath his stare. Flynae wraps her arms around herself as the trembling increases.

Her energy is constricted, withdrawn. He doesn't know if he should offer her his arm so he doesn't. She follows him as he leads the way out into the hallway.

As they walk to a room large enough for them to spar in, he notices again how little he can read from her. What does this mean for their ability to work together? Or create energy together?

Lord Thyde hears the sound of his footsteps echoing in her head. The grey corridors of his ship become the hallways they walked the night before. From her mind, he feels the tug of the collar against her neck and the jingle the chain makes in response.

Two memories overlap in her mind. In one moment, she remembers hanging by her wrists while he whips her and the Emperor watches with glee; in the next, her face is against a putrid-smelling pole, chained by her wrists, while Eksar assaults her from behind.

A whimper escapes her throat.

He pivots to see her lean her forehead and hand against the wall, suddenly overpowered by the nightmares of the past. Her body has become too weak to hold her up under the deluge of horrific images, sounds, and smells.

"Flynae," he softly calls. "Don't turn away from me. Please." Every heartbeat that passes while he sees her in this deep distress is agony.

Kovad doesn't want to approach her and force her to take solace in him though he aches to comfort her. *Baby. Please.*

That's enough to make her spin around to him. He drops to one knee; and she throws her arms around his shoulders, burying her face in his neck. Her tears wet his skin while her body trembles violently.

Her toes drive into the floor as her heels lift, pushing her weight against him as if she could somehow get even closer.

Everything he thinks of saying sounds so hollow. *I'm here. I've got you. You're safe.*

It all sounds like a lie. He might be with her now, but for how long?

Lord Thyde channels his helplessness and rage into his fist and clamps it down on her waist. If this is what she wants from him the most, then he can at least fulfill that.

The sudden pressure and pain take her breath away, making him wonder if it was too much. His fears are allayed as she begins to calm and stops crying.

If I'm with you, in person or in your mind, tell me what you need. I'll do anything within my power for you. Use me.

Her body stiffens. *Don't tell me things you might not mean in the future.*

For the first time in a long time, he's ashamed of his past.

She knows he'd already promised himself to another and then broke his word. She knows every moment of his life that he isn't proud of.

He hears her inhale and recognize his smell of regret.

Oh gods, I'm sorry. That was cruel. She nuzzles her face against him. *I'm terrified of how badly you could hurt me if you were to change your mind.*

It's okay. You don't need to apologize to me. With the hand that isn't holding her waist, he strokes her hair. *I don't deserve you. There isn't a soul alive that deserves you.*

His anger rises. Though she's starting to regain her composure, the violent quivering of her body hasn't abated. If he had the means, he would keep Eksar and Seko alive, chained, and confined for years while he slowly removed chunks from their body.

She shakes her head in protest of his thought. *That's awful.*

No. What they do to you is awful. They deserve a lifetime of torment.

Kovad?

Yes, baby.

She hesitates, and he realizes it's because she's about to ask for something but is still unsure.

It's okay. Tell me. Remember, you get anything you want, Flynae, he repeats what he told her in the vision.

Bruise me again? Her thought is timid and quiet.

He realizes his hand on her side has relaxed. He drops his other arm so that he can hold both sides.

After brushing aside his instinctual thought of displeasure at hurting her, he savagely clutches. Her breath comes out in a groan, but the calming effect on her body is near instantaneous. She relaxes into him, allowing him to hold her up, as her tremors lessen. The shivers don't stop altogether, but they're no longer as intense and debilitating. She sighs in relief.

"I think I can walk now." Her voice wavers a little. *Thank you.*

"Anything, Flynae."

When she steps back, he stands up. She slips her fingers through his, and he squeezes her hand.

17

E82 Evening (Kovad)

Flynae sighs when it's time to release him.

Lord Thyde notices how dark and tired her eyes are. The day is rapidly waning.

"Just a couple hours, Flynae." His voice has a slight begging tone to it.

She nods. "I'm fine."

They start with some sparring to test the new and newly upgraded lifeswords.

Kovad is astonished by how the weapon seems to flow with him and contribute to the movements instead of being a lifeless object. She tries to hide her smiles at his delight with it.

"You should be proud of yourself," he says.

She blushes and averts her eyes.

After an hour with the lifeswords, they practice the energy shields the way they did the last time they were at the ranch on Halaa together. They're each able to make their own and use them to block against the other's lifesword, but the shields won't combine the way they had fifteen months ago.

Kovad knows it's because of whatever defense she's built

in her mind to keep her emotions at bay. However much she might protest it, he understands they need to knock it down before they're separated again. He can't fully understand the trepidation it's causing him; but he knows that if she were being honest, she would agree.

When he thinks about it for the third time, she exhales loudly and drops her shoulders. "Fine. But can we do it tomorrow morning? I think we'll have a few hours."

His throat and chest constrict at the mention of their time together coming to an end. "Only a few? Do you see something?"

Flynae shakes her head. "Just a feeling. Like some impending doom approaching around eleven or twelve hundred hours." Her face tightens into a grimace, and she hugs herself as if suddenly cold. "But I just really can't face it tonight."

"Okay. I won't force it." Lord Thyde checks the time. "Come. We should eat so you can rest." His first instinct is to take her hand, but he resists and offers her his. If he gets to hold or touch her, it will be because she initiates the contact.

But what if I want to touch you, she asks as she places her hand in his.

"You get anything you want, Flynae."

Am I going to be hearing that a lot?

"It might be my new mantra."

He orders dinner brought to her sitting room so they can eat in front of her coffee table.

As soon as she enters, she sees two new additions to the right of the door. Across from the couch are two completely stocked wine fridges. One holds twenty bottles of white wine while the other holds twenty bottles of red.

"When did you have time to do this?" She spins around to look up at him.

"It was the first thing I did after our meal."

"How did you keep it a secret?"

"You were distracted with your lifesword. You should choose something to have with your dinner." He gives an encouraging nod.

Instead of moving towards the wine, she moves to him and hugs him. "You're spoiling me."

"Hardly." Kovad grasps her with one arm. He begins to bring his other hand up to caress her cheek but stops himself halfway. That isn't a liberty he's taken before, and he doesn't want to take any now. Instead, he hesitates and waits for any response from her.

Flynae reaches up and brings it to her face. Both a thrill and a tremor run through her. She mostly suppresses a whimper as she constricts under the intense emotions.

Kovad drops his hand to squeeze her shoulder. "It's okay. Let me earn it. What wine do you want tonight?"

With more than a little reluctance, she leaves his arms to inspect her newest gifts and select one.

When dinner and the first bottle of wine are finished, she sits at the piano and begins to play.

He notices no transformation like when she'd performed at the ranch. Instead, she almost seemed to shrink and diminish as if she were afraid of it.

Flynae sings and plays The Highwayman and Dante's Prayer. Kovad finds himself touched by the song's sentiments and her voice, but when he checks in with her energy, it is neutral. She isn't even feeling the songs the way she did before.

He listens for a little while longer before deciding to pull himself away. There are a few things that he should get done before going to bed, and he's hoping she'll be tired and sleep soon.

She pauses after the next song and stands up when he does.

"May I hug you?" The significance of the questions in the vision was not lost on him.

Please. She falls into him, her body melting into his.

Once he has his arms around her, it's difficult to release her, especially knowing he'll be leaving her for the night as soon as he does. The other option is to offer to sleep next to her, but that could be its own form of punishment for him. The safest thing to do is walk away.

"Sleep well, my lady."

"Good night, Lord Thyde."

She sits back down and continues playing as he leaves.

18

E83 Shower (Kovad)

Lord Thyde wakes up at 0200 with a burning need to check on her. How stupid was he to have left her alone? His heart races as he jumps up and walks across the hall in only his sleep pants.

When the door opens, he sees her across the room. Flynae's still sitting at the piano, sleeping with her head down on the closed cover.

Instantly, he feels bad as if he'd abandoned her. Of course, she wasn't going to be comfortable and get deep rest by herself. The three empty wine bottles on the floor near the piano bench lead him to believe she hasn't been asleep for long. *Baby, I need you to tell me how to take care of you.*

He advances to her side as quietly as he can and gently scoops her up.

Flynae cries out and jerks. Her legs thrash, and she pushes against him.

Not only was he not expecting this reaction, but he also didn't anticipate how physically strong she is. After nearly dropping her completely, Kovad releases her lower body and holds her torso with both arms. For added safety, he moves to his knee so her feet are on the floor. "I'm sorry. It's me. You're okay."

Flynae's heart pounds in her chest and ears. She struggles to regain control of her breathing. Her shoulders tense and lift. "What are you doing?" she pants.

"I was moving you to bed so you would be more comfortable and maybe get more restful sleep."

"I don't sleep in beds." Now that she knows where she is and who has her, Flynae leans her head against his shoulder and exhales with relief. "I don't sleep much."

"You'll sleep if I hold you, won't you?"

She nods. "Probably." She closes her eyes and inhales deeply, smelling his affection and concern.

"Then I apologize for not asking sooner." He carries her to the couch and reclines with her.

After just a few minutes, she's asleep again. Only then does he allow himself to drift off.

***

Kovad wakes up three hours later at his normal rising time of 0500. The first thing he notices is that he's now stretched out on the couch, and she's mostly on top of him. His body hums with bliss as he notices her gentle weight.

Her head and hand rest on his bare chest. Her torso is against his. One of her legs lies between his, while his erection presses against her thigh.

He tenses when he notices how aroused he is.

Fuck. I don't want her to wake up with me like a horny teenager who can't control his body. The vision from yesterday must have affected him more than he thought, and the pressure of her body against him is intoxicating. *How do I get up without waking her?*

The best option he comes up with in his distress at feeling he'd already assaulted her is to gently roll her away while he slides off the couch. First, he coaxes her leg most of the way off him. He rotates his torso to push her back into the couch.

Flynae jerks upright and away, her eyelids blinking several times. Her eyes are heavy from sleep and only halfway open when she looks at him. "What?"

He turns away from her. The loose pants he's wearing offer no way to disguise what's happening. "I didn't mean to wake you. I'll be back in a little bit."

She inhales.

"Why are you flustered?" She evaluates his scent again. *Because you're aroused? Oh.* Everything he saw and felt right after waking comes to her. *I didn't mean–*

Kovad shakes his head as he walks from the room, irritated at why he had to wake her and then walk out on her. *It's not your fault, Flynae. You didn't do anything. I just need a minute.* The sound of her voice in his head is enough to make his body ache and throb even more.

Within moments, he's naked beneath a cold stream of water in his shower and focusing on his breath. He still feels her against him. He remembers how she tasted in the vision. All he wants right now is to hold her and never let her go. None of these thoughts help his erection go down.

Lord Thyde groans in frustration at his current lack of control. To distract himself even more, he begins running through the recent reports he needs to review.

When he feels warm water flowing over her skin and knows that she's naked in a shower across the hall, his body becomes more excited with desire for her. He turns his water even colder and continues thinking about work.

A few minutes later, Kovad's close to shivering; but it finally feels safe to turn off the water and get out. He dries off and gets dressed before reaching out energetically to see if she's finished her shower yet. What he discovers makes him swear under his breath.

When she had gone to rinse off, she hadn't turned on the light in the room. Now she's sitting in a pitch-black corner of the tile shower, naked and trembling. She'd switched off the water as she sank to the floor.

What are you doing, Flynae? The question is more rhetorical than directed at her to answer. He hurries across the hallway and leans his forehead against her bathroom door. *How am I supposed to get to you?*

I–I can't move. I started thinking about today and....

Kovad hears her single sob through her ears. *I'm coming to get you.*

I'm not dressed.

I'll bring a towel to wrap you in and leave the light off.

He waits for her object. When she doesn't respond, he opens the door and steps inside the room with her. He takes a moment to note the towel rack and shower entrance in the triangle of light before enclosing them both in pitch blackness. Keeping his hand against the wall, he moves along it to the right. He collects the oversized plush towel and continues.

Flynae's nearly silent as she listens and waits for him.

Finally, he's next to her, wrapping her in the towel, and helping her to stand. The violent trembling of her body pains him. He wants to scream and rage at his inability to make a difference for her.

She wiggles one of her arms free of the towel and touches his neck. "Don't torment yourself. Just be here."

Lord Thyde marvels at her bravery and concern for him amid her implosion. He holds her tightly while beginning to feel for the wall to guide them out.

"Wait." She turns her hand palm up between them. A four-inch flame appears just above the skin of her hand. Her eyes glint and shine in the glow of the warm light.

He wonders if she'll ever stop surprising him. "When did you learn to do that?"

"Just a few months ago."

"You're amazing, Flynae."

She doesn't respond.

When he moves and she tries to walk with him, her legs almost give out on her again.

His first instinct is just to lift her into his arms, but he remembers how well that went earlier this morning. He opens his mouth to tell her that he's going to pick her up and then recalls the vision. "May I carry you?"

"Yes." *Thank you for asking.*

Lord Thyde effortlessly lifts her off her feet and takes her from the room while she lights the way. He sits on the edge of her bed and grips her tightly until her tremors calm.

After a few minutes, she tries to hide a yawn.

"Can you walk?"

"I think so."

"Why don't you get dressed and meet me out on the couch? I'll sit with you while you get more sleep."

She presses her head against his shoulder. "Our time is short."

"You've had little more than three hours of sleep. You're exhausted. Just a couple more hours."

"Okay."

He helps her find her feet before leaving the room.

When she comes out, Flynae stumbles about like she's sleepwalking. She plops down onto the sofa and leans into him. Within just a few minutes, she's asleep again.

19

E84 The Construct Part 1 (Kovad)

As her body gets heavier, he helps her lay down. Flynae settles her head on his thigh. Kovad strokes her hair and upper arm as he works. Every time he looks down at her sleeping face, he can't help but think about how much he wants this to be the rest of his life.

He only got her back in his head less than thirty-six hours ago. Now all he wants is to be near her. Her presence is the only thing he's ever craved.

Despite how Flynae keeps her emotions locked away, everything about her is more intense than ever before. When he looks at her, her beauty takes his breath away. His body hungers for contact with her skin.

With a sigh, Lord Thyde returns his focus to the screen before him to avoid requiring a second cold shower that morning.

She wakes a couple of hours later. He watches her thoughts as she becomes aware of where she is. Her body responds with a rush once she's mostly conscious.

Flynae sits up and moves against him. He hears her inhale and feels her relish his scent.

Without much forethought or warning, she climbs onto his lap. He quickly pushes the computer out of her way and wraps her in his arms.

I missed you. She nuzzles her face against his neck.

The image of her naked body hanging by chains rushes to the forefront of his mind. For a few seconds, Kovad gives in to the agony of the memory. Within another moment, he realizes she's crying. He aches to kiss her head.

I missed you, too, Flynae. So much. He tightens his arms around her.

We're running out of time. She presses into him. *We need to do this.*

As if in preparation for what she's proposing, her body shakes. Her delicate little fingers dig into Kovad's arm as she holds on to him.

Care and rage run through him in equal measure. This must be purgatory. He killed an immortal and watching what he wants to protect the most suffer is his punishment.

Flynae's hand on his face, turning it towards her, causes his eyes to meet hers. Her large, emerald eyes are wide with concern. She shakes her head. *Don't think that.*

Kovad soaks in the view of her face: from her perfect marble white skin and pixie-like nose to her soft pink lips.

She blushes and suddenly stands. *Can we get this over with?*

Yes. His body tenses with dread. This will be painful for both of them but especially for her. He isn't looking forward to it.

They walk back to the room where they trained before. The open space seems more appropriate for the work that's required.

Flynae backs up against him, and he holds her as he did that day at the ranch fifteen months prior. One arm is across her stomach, holding her waist. The other sits over her collarbone, holding her bicep.

Her body trembles more violently as if in protest. He tightens his hold on her.

Her side is already bruised from the day before, and he feels the pain she does from his touch. For a moment, he loosens his grasp.

No! Don't hold back. Her heart pounds even faster.

I don't want to hurt you. He sees and hears the whip in a memory as he strikes her back two days past. His hands tighten. *I never wanted to hurt you.* He presses his face against the side of her head.

I know. Her hands come up to hold onto his forearm. *I need you. Please be strong for me.*

His fingers dig into her side.

Her body leans into his. *Yes.*

Kovad goes to Flynae in her mind. She stands waiting in front of the locked closet door. When he approaches, she drops her head and twists her fingers together in front of her body.

He holds out his hand close enough to her that she'll see it.

You know exactly how to get to me. She places her hand in his and lifts her eyes. *I love that about you.*

I love everything about you. The thought happens naturally in response to her words. There is no place to hide when it comes to the mind link.

Are you ready?

Flynae's body tenses in opposition. *As ready as I'll ever be.*

When he walks to the door, she has no choice but to follow him as she's unwilling to release him.

When he places his hand over the doorknob, she tugs on him, making him pause.

Once we start this, we can't stop. This strong feeling sits like a rock in her gut. *Promise me that you'll see this through.*

He sees briefly all the pain she's holding back, all the pain she's carrying alone. It will continue to be a weight exclusively on her if they don't break down the barriers she built. *I promise. I won't fail you, my lady. Baby. What else do you need to hear?*

She hesitates once more. He feels the physical lump in her throat.

Don't be angry.

His temper blooms in response. *At who?* He knows this journey is only going to fuel his rage at Eksar.

Flynae cowers. *At me.*

He pulls her mental being into his arms. *Why would I ever be angry at you? I can't imagine anything you would do to cause that.*

Her small delicate fingers grip him in both their shared mental space and physically. Her body writhes against him. *I didn't know how else to cope. I was unprepared to be without you.*

He holds her even tighter.

She releases a gasp and relaxes into him a little.

It's okay. Whatever it is that you're afraid of–. He evaluates what she's feeling. *Whatever you're ashamed of. It's okay. I won't be angry at you.*

Knowing that it's now or never, he opens the door.

20

E85 The Construct, Part 2 (Kovad)

Before them spreads out a long metal corridor. Lord Thyde feels the Emperor jerking the collar about her neck. All Flynae's trepidation that she'd suppressed comes flooding into the memory. She'd been mortified when Seko had stripped her in front of Lord Thyde. The humiliation continued when he then raped her.

She was a piece of garbage that Eksar and Seko used and discarded. How would Kovad ever desire her after watching what they did to her? All she wanted was someone to cherish her, but each day contributes to her feelings of being refuse.

In her memory, she only felt gratitude towards Lord Thyde when he whipped her. He had saved her from permanent disfigurement.

Kovad's emotion about that night encroaches as a great boulder ready to crush them both. It was like his worst nightmare had materialized. The horror of that night sits against his shoulders like a great weight.

If you want to head back, now is the time. When Flynae looks at him, there's no judgment on her face. *I understand.*

No. No part of him can leave her like this, dealing with her emotions on her own. She'd endured this for fifteen months without him. He doesn't want her to carry this alone a moment longer.

Lord Thyde sets his shoulders. The intensity of what they're facing momentarily surprised him. From here forward, he needs to focus on her. She's the only thing that matters.

Before them, the metal corridor stretches out. Echoing down the hallways is the rattle of chains and Flynae's gasps. He involuntarily tenses. This was something he'd never wanted to relive.

Flynae squeezes his hand. *I'm here.*

Kovad realizes she'd gotten them both through that nightmare with the Emperor. He'd almost frozen and caused her permanent injury.

You have always been so strong. From the beginning, he admired her strength. *I don't deserve you.* The thought slips out without permission. But thoughts never ask permission. They've both shared things through the mindlink that they might not otherwise say, like the way he can't help but call her baby in his mind.

Then who does? She turns and faces the hallways of misery before them. *I can't face this with anyone else.* Her quietest of thoughts whispers, *I love you.*

He steps into the corridor. The echoes of his footsteps assault his ears. They're even louder than he remembered. Then he realizes that he's hearing them through her ears. All the senses are from her memory.

Flynae had been terrified, yet she'd held her head high and had kept walking knowing that some hell of the Emperor's creation was waiting for them.

When Seko had raped her, the emotion she had suppressed and hidden the most was shame. How would Kovad ever want her if another defiled her in front of him?

Lord Thyde notices the repeating thought. This is the second time in short succession that she's worried about becoming undesirable to him. Knowing that Flynae feels that way makes his stomach ill. Why would that thought cross her mind?

The rage he felt when he threw the whip away that night returns. It's his turn to subdue his emotions. Now is not the time for him to lose control. This is about Flynae.

Lord Thyde continues on, dragging her past the room where his past self is uncuffing her bloody wrists.

The next room is like a dark sanitarium. The smell of a strong alkaline cleaner assaults his nose. The ceiling lights flicker. A heart rate monitor beeps.

Kovad sees Flynae strapped to a hospital bed. She's hooked up to several monitors. An i.v. needle is in her hand. The beeping quickens as she becomes aware of Eksar's presence as he enters.

Eksar leans over her, close enough that his hot breath assaults her face. "It looks like your part in these little experiments are over for now. Seko wants you back next week. You'll be performing for him at a banquet."

Her initial response to his words was relief until he mentioned the Emperor. Every few days, for the past fifteen months, she'd been subjected to extractions or injections. Sometimes, she was sick for weeks afterward, barely able to walk or stand. Every time Eksar saw her in a debilitated state, she would smell the sickly, foul scent of his twisted pleasure.

That smell washes over her now as she lies helpless on the bed.

Eksar removes his pants and straddles her. "Between now and then, I'm to see that you are unblemished."

The room around Flynae fades. Instead of Eksar above her, she sees Kovad.

Lord Thyde watches the memory of her fantasy. Emotions rapidly fire through him. Outrage. Hate. Sadness. Affection. Anguish. Loathing.

The Flynae in the reverie pulls him to her. Their lips meet.

Her body in the recollection cries out and jerks in pain. She focuses more deeply on the daydream.

Flynae's physical body jerks in his arms. He has to release her as she turns around so that she can bury her face against him.

Kovad notices how shaky her legs are. He supports her weight while lowering them to sit on the floor and pulls her into his lap.

"I'm sorry." Her voice is barely a whisper.

He only understands what she says from hearing her in his head; her words are low and muffled. "What do you have to be sorry about?"

As if in response, Kovad feels her craving for him. Without his help, Flynae had been unable to create a safe place in her mind to hide from the trauma. She couldn't stand the reality of Eksar touching her and had preferred to pretend she was with Kovad instead.

She lifts a hand to her head, and her neatly trimmed claws dig into her scalp as if she could pull the painful past out that way.

Kovad takes her hand and brings it to his lips. "You don't need to apologize."

21

E86 The Construct, Part 3 (Kovad)

The dark hospital room fades. It's replaced with the small, plain bedroom she lived in on Moki. Eksar carries her to the bed and throws her down on it.

Sekara runs in after him, tears streaming down her face. "Let her go." She tries to pull him away from her sister.

A loud smack echos off the wood walls as Eksar slaps Sekara. Flynae jumps up to stand between him and Sekara and begins pushing her twin back towards the door.

Eksar grabs Flynae and yanks her back.

"Please go," Flynae begs Sekara.

After a body-shuddering sob, Sekara turns and flees.

Eksar ruthlessly claws her clothes from her, shredding the fabric and leaving long red marks on her torso.

Flynae covers her face with her hands but is too worn out to resist or fight back. Resistance has only been futile.

He shoves her face down onto the bed and climbs onto her.

Everything real fades. Now it's Kovad's weight on her. He kisses her neck. Her body melts into his.

She immerses herself in the fantasy until Eksar's voice

growls in her ear. "You would be wise to not make me angry. You don't think I can make this worse on you, but you're wrong."

His hand moves down her front to between her legs and begins viciously rubbing. The pressure creates a painful, burning sensation that spreads into her torso.

As much as she tries not to, Flynae begins crying. "Please! Stop!" she begs. Her body instinctively bucks against him.

Eksar laughs in and continues tormenting her clit. Her body shakes and shudders as the agony builds.

There is no retreating back into her fantasy from this new torture. She tries to conjure up old memories, feelings of Kovad holding her before. Nothing sticks. Her mind keeps coming back to the piercing pain like a hot knife between her legs.

Eksar doesn't relent until the feeling builds into an excruciating climax. As she sobs into her pillow, she's barely aware of his weight lifting from her body.

Kovad comes back to the present as Flynae shifts in his lap. She sits up, bringing her face next to his, her mouth next to his ear.

"I want you." Her lips brush against him as she speaks softly.

Lord Thyde's body twists into knots. He's trying to control his horror at how cruel Eksar has been to Flynae, while Flynae is overwhelmed with suppressed emotions of love and lust for him.

"Flynae." He shakes his head, struggling for words. Not finding any, he sighs.

Her body stiffens in his arms. "You don't want me?"

Kovad suppresses a despairing groan. "Of course, I want you. But it's not appropriate."

"What happened to anything? Everything?" Hurt and anger

fill her tone now.

He tightens his hold on her. "Please don't ask for something that would make me despise myself."

Flynae's intensity breaks, and she collapses against him again. *Why?* She begins sobbing. *Why can they take whatever they want from me, but I can't give it to you?*

Tears spill down his cheeks. *What they do to you is awful, baby. And even if you wanted to give your body willingly to me now, I would still feel like I was taking advantage of your youth and trauma.*

She begins constricting, physically and emotionally. She draws her knees up to her chest, her feet resting on his thigh. *I'm sorry.* Her thought is a whimper as her body breaks out in violent, trembling shivers.

Not knowing what else to do or say, he just holds her. They have to go back into her memories, and he's dreading it. Dreading both knowing what she endured on her own and making her relive it.

They move to the next room. Flynae is restrained to a hospital bed. Someone takes a blood sample from her. Another person injects something into her arm. As the chemical spreads through her body, it causes excruciating pain. From behind nearby doors, creatures shriek, responding to her cries.

The memory is thankfully short but leaves him with a lot of unanswered questions.

He watches her run to the library every chance she can and pull up the most recent news videos that might show his face.

Everything intensifies the further back they go, the closer they get to when they were first separated. Her emotions are sharper, rawer.

Kovad watches Eksar carry her in from creating the slave

mark on her shoulder. When Eksar begins to assault her, Flynae feels Kovad bruising her that morning at the ranch.

When the violation is over, everything fades away from in front of them except for a small wooden chest. Kovad remembers watching Flynae tell her younger self not to cry before and realizes what has been locked away. She'd put the part of her that remained a hurt, little child into the box. To make it worse, she'd created a slot in the top to stuff every emotion she couldn't handle inside as well.

She braces as he approaches the chest. She wants him to just leave it alone.

Flynae. You told me to see this through.

No, no, no. She falls to her knees in their shared mental space. *I can't.*

She grabs his ankle.

The sight of her nearly prostrate at his feet overwhelms him.

He's torn. *You told me we can't stop.* Her begging is overwhelming and heartbreaking.

He kneels down and pulls her into his arms. *I have you. Let me open that box and comfort all of you.*

When she doesn't resist, he opens the chest. It's deeper than it looks on the outside. About five feet down is a four-year-old Flynae. Her dress is dark brown with dirt. Her green eyes glint up at him from within a soiled face. They're the only thing that shines from within the chest.

His arms are empty for a moment as he reaches in and picks up the child within. She morphs with her other half and becomes one.

Everything collides at once. He hears her verbally cry out in anguish. All the emotions crash into her at once. He squeezes her tighter as she jerks and thrashes.

Flynae screams. Her body writhes with the torment of stifled memories and heaves with every breath.

All he knows to do is grip her tighter.

I have you. It's okay.

After several painful moments, she stills and sits there quietly crying.

He wants to do anything to comfort further. *May I kiss your head?*

Yes.

He lowers his lips to her head and lets them linger there.

22

E87 Collected (Flynae)

Flynae shivers in Lord Thyde's lap, huddled into as small of a ball as she can be. The tidal wave of suppressed emotions devastates and overwhelms her. Many of the horrifying details of the last fifteen months had been hidden from her conscious mind behind the mental barrier she'd built. Now, all at the same time, she experiences them all again like it's the first time. The feelings of being used and tossed to the side like trash are some of the worst to endure again.

She takes a deep breath and analyzes Lord Thyde's scent. Lingering under the surface, the most foul-smelling feelings are restrained. The strongest aromas are comforting more than anything. Worry, care, and affection are the most prominent.

The gentle pressure of his lips on her head brings her solace. Someone wants her. The most important person wants her. His is the only opinion that matters.

Flynae leans into him and begins to relax a little.

If only it could be just the two of them, hidden away from the rest of the universe's madness in their own safe little bubble. She heightens the feeling of being sheltered away and safe with just him.

Something catches his attention and causes him to open his eyes.

She mourns the decrease in contact as he lifts his head.

Kovad gasps.

"Flynae," he whispers, giving her two short pulsing squeezes. "Open your eyes."

With slight reluctance, she looks at what has caught his attention. It's her turn to gasp.

A great energy shield surrounds them. It's bigger and more beautiful than any she has witnessed before.

The dome is made of dazzling warm white light that glitters and glints with all the colors. The outlines of it remind her of the fields of a magnet. The shield is slightly flattened near the top before it flows out in a complete circle around them.

Flynae moves from his lap, and Lord Thyde stands up with her. She leans her back against him, and he puts his arms around her.

The shield expands to accommodate them. The top of it maintains a constant distance of roughly a foot above Kovad's head.

Her slight intention maintains the shimmering energy effortlessly.

"How?" Flynae looks up at Lord Thyde.

Kovad lifts his eyebrows and shakes his head in puzzlement. "It's all you, Flynae."

"It can't be. I can't do this on my own." She extends her arm and touches it. The energy is firm like a wall, but it expands and adjusts to her as she presses against it.

"Except that you are." He leans down and kisses her head again.

When his lips touch her hair, the energy shield brightens, almost blindingly so.

"You're the catalyst." She tilts to make eye contact with him again. "You're my catalyst."

For a few moments, they stay like that, focusing on each other.

A thrill builds in her core. She wants to ask him to bend down and kiss her. Her lips part as she considers giving her thoughts a voice.

Kovad's mind betrays him, revealing that if she were to ask, he wouldn't say no.

Time feels suspended as she considers. Was it so wrong for her to want this?

Flynae inhales again and catches a slight trace of Kovad's desire for her. She realizes it's been there the whole time this past day and a half. He's kept the majority of it constrained. All she can detect is the tip of the iceberg.

Again, his thoughts disclose his secrets, baring them for her to see. Since he first laid eyes on her two days ago, he can't get the idea and image of kissing her out of his head. He continually pushes them away, hiding them, so as not to pressure her to do anything that wasn't her idea first.

Flynae's left shoulder tingles. She pushes herself away from Lord Thyde, leaving him surprised and confused.

The energy bubble disappears.

Her heart races. Panic grips her throat and chest, making breathing difficult.

Flynae fumbles with her belt. In her haste and fright, her fingers won't cooperate. Finally, she frees it from her and slides the belt with her lifesword attached across the room to rest against the wall.

"What are you doing?" Kovad whispers.

"Eksar's coming." She turns to him and pleads with her eyes. "Please don't engage him. Don't give him reason to hurt you."

Kovad's anger flares. His hands clench into shaking fists. *I'm supposed to stand back while he hurts you?* "Why? What about the shield? That must be stronger than anything he can do."

Kovad takes a step towards her, and Flynae takes a step back, shaking her head.

"It won't work." She flattens her palms together in a praying motion and brings her index fingers to her lips. *Please, Kovad. I need you to stay safe.*

"Why? I just watched you work more magic than I ever thought possible. Give me a good reason why you aren't using it against him now?"

The drumbeat of Lord Thyde's heart pounds in her ears. She smells his confusion and frustration as much as she experiences them with him through the link.

Flynae shakes her head and allows it to fall forward. Her hands drop to her sides.

"Because nothing I can do matters when it comes to Eksar right now. I can't–" Her words are cut off by a cry of pain as she crumples to the floor. A rush of pain floods through her nerves radiating out from the mark on her shoulder.

Through the agony, she's vaguely aware of Eksar entering the room and Lord Thyde rushing to her. Kovad is blocked from reaching her and pushed back by a wall of energy.

"I just don't understand the Emperor's fascination with humans." Eksar's tone is mocking. He shakes his head and turns to Flynae. "I can at least almost understand yours. Seeing as how your pathetic uncle is obsessed with them."

As soon as the pain subsides a little, Flynae gasps for breath.

There are multiple levels of pain Eksar can inflict through the slave mark. This one wasn't the worst of them, but it was debilitating.

She attempts to push herself off the floor but can't manage to lift her head. When he wants to incapacitate her, as he has done now, it can take hours or even a full day for her to regain the strength to stand. It's like all the energy has been squeezed from every muscle and cell in her body. Even breathing is difficult.

With a sigh, Eksar bends down and throws her over his shoulder. "The Emperor is ready for his toy back. Though she's in surprisingly better condition than I expected. Very curious."

Without another word, he carries her away.

She sees through Lord Thyde's eyes as Kovad watches Eksar leave with her. In his grief, the human hyper-focuses on her long red hair as it nearly drags on the floor.

23

E88 Closet Conversation (Flynae)

Flynae's heart hammers against the confines of her ribcage as the door to the shuttle closes behind them, sealing her inside with Eksar.

He orders his pilot to set their course to The Dominion before depositing her in a heap in a corner on the floor.

Trash, she thinks.

You're not trash, Flynae.

You're still here. Tears come unbidden to her eyes. She clings to Kovad's mental form in their space. *I'm so grateful you're still here.*

As am I, baby.

Flynae dozes for most of the flight as her exhausted body tries to recover.

Rough hands awaken her. Eksar lifts and slings her over his shoulder again.

He throws her down on a bed instead of the floor this time. She cowers under his hateful gaze.

"This," Eksar begins ripping her dress off, "is not proper attire for your station."

A moment later, she's in a ball on the mattress wearing only dance shorts.

"I thought Seko said he made Lord Thyde whip you," Eksar muses. "Where are the marks?"

Flynae chokes on her panic as she waits for Eksar to assault her, but he leaves her alone instead. When the door closes behind him, she takes a moment to mourn the loss of the dress Lord Thyde had given her. It didn't matter that he had bought her dozens of them. She cherished each one and the thought that went into it as if it were the only one.

With what little strength returned, Flynae pushes herself into a sitting position. She recognizes the simple yet elegant decor that runs throughout the entirety of the living quarters of the Emperor's harem. The walls are grey with black and gold accents.

A shiver runs through her. She pulls the top blanket from the bed around her for warmth and a covering.

The door Eksar left through taunts her. Seko or Eksar could walk through at any moment. She's here for Seko's pleasure any time he wants it.

The room is suddenly too big and open. It's difficult for her to catch her breath. She swings her legs off the bed and lowers herself to the floor. From there, she crawls to the other door in the room which she assumes leads to a closet. Her suspicions are confirmed when she opens it.

Hanging within are dresses and outfits that she presumes will fit her. It's obvious from the lack of material, that each one is more revealing than anything Lord Thyde bought for her.

She drags herself inside and closes the door behind her. The dark, enclosed space is much easier to deal with than the wide open room.

She leans against the wall and takes a few deep breaths. *Kovad?*

I'm here, Flynae.

His voice in her head brings her a little comfort. She gravitates to his mental presence.

Muffled voices to her left catch her attention. She places her ear against the cold metal wall to see if she can hear what they're saying.

"I thought you said you made him whip her," Eksar says.

"I did," Seko replies. The glee in his voice is unmistakable. "She was a bloody mess when Lord Thyde was done with her. And then I took her right in front of him. You should have felt his distress." Seko releases a pleased sigh before his tone changes to a mutter. "Although you would have been able to smell it. I can only imagine how delicious it was. He really is smitten with her."

Eksar's response is nonchalant. "Well, she doesn't have a mark on her."

"What? That's impossible. Even skilled healers don't completely heal anyone that quickly. Hmm." The Emperor sounds legitimately puzzled. "Wait," he says sharply. "How do you know she doesn't have a mark?"

"I stripped her and looked."

The Emperor's voice is low and stern. "I told you not to touch her. She's no longer yours to do what you want with."

"Relax. All I did was undress her. I didn't fondle your toy; I showed restraint."

Flynae's stomach lurches. She can't imagine Eksar maintaining any sort of restraint towards her for long.

"As you will in the future. Now you will transfer her slave mark to me."

"No." Eksar's single word hangs in the air unanswered for a moment.

She imagines Seko leaning forward to respond.

"What do you mean no?"

"If I release her mark to you, you don't need me here. You'll send me back to Moki or some other gods-awful place. I plan to stick around for a while."

Flynae thinks Eksar sounds like he's smirking with delight. He's found a way to hold something over the Emperor.

"Don't cross me, Eksar. There's more than one way to transfer a slave mark."

Transfer. The word jumps out to Flynae.

"I don't think I'm your immediate problem. I think you need to keep her away from Lord Thyde. The two of them were–training, I think. Maybe he's outlived his usefulness."

Flynae's breath catches. *No, no, no.*

"I will be the one to decide that," Seko snaps. "You will leave them both alone for the time being. I suppose I'll have quarters prepared for you since you want to be responsible for my royal prize."

Flynae listens for a little while longer, but she hears no further discourse. Fatigue eventually overtakes her, and she falls asleep.

24

E89 Respect (Flynae)

Flynae's body is heavy when she drags herself from the closet signaling that she'd been asleep for a while. She tenses when the first thought she has is checking the mindlink.

Kovad? She braces, expecting to hear nothing in response.

I'm here, Flynae.

Tears of relief slide down her face. *I'm so afraid of losing you again.*

I know, baby. I am, too.

His words warm and comfort her.

Flynae stands. Her body is stiff and still a little weak, but walking is possible without too much effort. She begins looking through her clothing selection. Everything in the closet is designed to show a lot of skin. She selects a bandeau crop top and harem pants with a slit on both sides from the waistband to the ankles. They're the most casual options available.

Only a few moments after she's dressed, she hears a commotion and someone crying nearby. With her heart in her throat, she leaves the room to investigate.

The next room has what looks like four bedroom doors, including the one she came from, that open onto it. To the left is a round window with a cushioned bench, looking out into space. To the right is a large archway leading into the central foyer of the harem quarters.

The foyer is a large room with a vaulted ceiling. A circular fountain graces the middle of the open space. The crying comes from the other side of the fountain.

When Flynae enters the foyer, she recognizes one of the Kaliah women from her previous visit. The Kaliah has dark brown hair and amber eyes. She stands with a small crowd of attractive human women. The human ages probably range from sixteen to twenty-six.

The group of six stands watching another human female who lies on the floor sobbing. The girl on the floor is naked and covered with bruises. Blood streaks down her legs and pools beneath the lower part of her torso.

Flynae stands there for another moment, taking in the scene and smells. The Kaliah smells dispassionate. The humans smell relieved and mildly entertained. She imagines they're glad it wasn't them this time. Amusement must be difficult to come by here if they're treating this like a show.

Flynae draws herself up to her full height of all of five feet two inches and pulls her shoulders back. "Really?" Her voice is stern and commanding.

All the onlookers blush, including the Kaliah, who meets her eyes and then looks away with an air of disdain.

Flynae walks to the human on the floor, kneels next to her, and pulls her into her arms. She allows calming energy to flow from her into the injured human.

The girl grips and clings to Flynae. Flynae holds her while

she continues to sob.

The circumstances are all too obvious to Flynae. The girl must be relatively new to the harem. Her smell is one of surprise and horror. She'd been taken off guard by the Emperor's brutality.

Flynae sits there patiently, holding the girl and stroking her light brown hair. She doesn't have any soothing words, but her actions are enough to begin to calm the girl.

"All right," Flynae says after a few minutes, "let's get you cleaned up and dressed, okay?"

The crying girl nods her head but doesn't otherwise move.

With a great effort from her still tired legs, Flynae gets them both to their feet. The human is about four inches taller than Flynae and continues to lean against her with most of her weight.

One of the other women comes forward with hesitant steps and makes eye contact. "How can I help?"

"What's your name?"

"Jasna." Beneath a swirl of long golden blonde hair, brilliant blue eyes appraise Flynae.

"Jasna, would you please start a bath?"

Jasna curtseys and hurries to do as she's asked.

As Flynae supports the crying girl towards the bathing room, the onlookers tiptoe after them. The overall emotions in the room are changing. She catches traces of awe and respect now.

By the time she gets the girl into the bathroom, steam is rising from the water filling the tub.

"Thank you, Jasna. Do you know her name?" Flynae inclines her head towards the girl in her arms.

"I think it's Bethany. She was just brought here two days ago."

"Is your name Bethany?" Flynae asks the brunette.

Bethany nods her affirmation.

Flynae supports the girl to the edge of the walk-in tub, but Bethany won't let go of her even when they stand at the edge. After only a moment's hesitation, Flynae continues, fully dressed, into the tub with the girl.

Her foot falters with fatigue, but strong hands grab her waist and steady her. As she turns around to sit down, Flynae finds herself looking up into the face of the dark-haired Kaliah who had been watching in the foyer.

"Thank you," Flynae says.

The Kaliah nods her head while closing her eyes in respect.

One of the other girls brings bath oils to pour into the water and hands Flynae a natural sea sponge. The humans and the Kaliah sit nearby, content and entranced by Flynae's calming aura, while Flynae gently washes the battered girl.

More and more women from the harem join them, drawn by Flynae's presence. Even the other Kaliah comes in and stands near the doorway.

Monarch. The word comes unbidden to Flynae's mind. *No. This doesn't mean anything. No one here is kind to anyone else. That's all. Not that I blame them.*

Bethany is calm by the time Flynae has her cleaned.

"All right. Let's get you dry and dressed," Flynae says softly, trying to keep her exhaustion from her voice. Being strong for all the tumultuous energies in the room has drained her. Still, she doesn't falter as she helps Bethany to her feet.

The second Kaliah comes over with a large towel to receive the girl with.

Flynae meets her eyes. "Don't leave her alone."

The Kaliah acknowledges the command with a quick bob of

her head. “Understood, royal daughter.” She wraps Bethany up and helps her out.

When Flynae turns to climb out of the tub, the other Kaliah is holding a towel for her. Someone brings a chair for her to sit down. Suddenly, she’s surrounded. Someone is drying her hair. Someone else has brought her a change of fresh clothes similar to what she’s wearing for her to approve or reject.

Within a few moments, they have her dry and dressed and are helping her back to her room. She sighs with relief as she lays on the bed.

Jasna brings a glass of water and a glass of red wine and places them on her nightstand.

Following the lead of the dark-haired Kaliah, the humans back their way out of her room, closing the door behind them.

Kovad? Now that she’s alone, the grief and trauma of the last hour inundate her. Tears spill down her cheeks. She curls into a ball and hugs her knees.

I’m here. His pride and admiration wash over her.

I need you.

He meets her in their shared space and wraps her mental being with his.

25

E90 Kneel (Flynae)

Flynae awakes from her nap feeling as if her strength is renewed. The first thought that enters her head when she notices Kovad's presence in her mind is, *I need you.*

I'm here, he replies reassuringly. *What else can I do?*

I just meant in general. I need you. I need you in my life. Everyday. The thoughts spill out faster than her ability to stop or censor them.

At first, he's speechless, overcome by feelings of helplessness. She watches him disregard thoughts, one after the other: *I want that. I want to give you everything. I'll promise you everything.* His lack of power and influence in this area turns to infuriation.

Tell me what to do, Flynae. You keep telling me what not to do. I'm trying to respect that. Each time you've proven to be right. But you haven't told me what I can do.

She mentally leans into him, completely unintimidated by his passionate response. *You're right. I haven't. But I have the beginnings of a thought. I just need a little more time.*

Whatever you require, my lady. I'll do anything for you.

Am I no longer baby? She catches herself pouting with disappointment not knowing what's changed. Had she done something wrong?

Of course, you are. You're everything to me. My lady. Baby. He laughs lightly, but not unkindly. *Besides. You're the one who has kept things formal. You haven't ever addressed me by my first name aloud.*

He wasn't wrong. She couldn't help but call him Kovad in her mind, mostly because that was how the voice in her head first introduced itself. But she always vocally addressed him by Lord Thyde or my lord whether in public or in private.

I know. But you haven't told me you love me. And I don't know what that means. Her thought pours out without permission as thoughts are want to do.

He's about ready to respond when the bedroom door flies open. The dark-haired Kaliah stands halfway in the doorway.

"The Emperor is here."

Flynae stares blankly at her but doesn't move.

"We're expected to receive him. All of us."

Flynae at first doesn't respond. Then she smells the Kaliah's worry.

"Please come out here," the Kaliah whispers the plea before disappearing from view.

Flynae stands and walks without hurrying out into the foyer.

Emperor Seko is eyeing each female in turn, inspecting their attire and figures for the day, while the girl or woman stands with a lowered head. When he is finished with one, he signals with a wave of his hand, and she drops to her knees.

Flynae stops short of joining the circle. Eventually, Seko's gaze makes its way to her. His eyes narrow when he sees her set face staring back at him.

He walks through the gap left for her in the semi-circle. "Kneel," he commands through gritted teeth.

Flynae raises her chin slightly in continued defiance.

"Kneel." He begins exerting pressure made of energy above her head, adding weight to her body.

She resists, pushing back against him.

What are you doing? Kovad asks in alarm.

Testing his strength. I need to know what I'm–we're up against.

The Emperor continues to pile on density.

You're going to get yourself hurt. Lord Thyde can't conceal his concern.

Pain is inevitable. We need the information.

Her body begins to quiver under the strain of the increasing strength of the Emperor.

Let me help.

No! He can't sense the mindlink. He can't know how connected we are. The distress of possibly putting him in more danger distracts her. Her legs give out, overwhelmed by the Emperor's stronger, ancient energy. But not before she caught a glimpse of the magnitude of it.

A banging noise echoes throughout the living quarters as her knees hit the ground.

Flynae closes her eyes and purses her lips to stop from crying out as her bones crack from the force exerted on her.

The Emperor smells of smug satisfaction and just a hint of alarm. Flynae hones in on this drop of weakness.

"You will kneel like the others," he says before moving on.

The pain radiates up through her core. Flynae's forehead breaks out in a sweat, but she doesn't move. She waits until he's finished his inspection, selected a girl to accompany him, and walks from the room. She delays while his energy fades down the hall. She doesn't want him to hear.

All eyes turn to her, as she leans to one side and cries out in agony. Daggers of pain shoot out from her knees. She tumbles over.

Within moments, many soft hands are grasping her, lifting her as carefully as possible, and carrying her to her bed.

Someone sets and straightens her legs. Another girl wipes her brow.

Flynae recognizes the voice of the dark-haired Kaliah directing the women to stand around Flynae.

"Give. Contribute. The knowing doesn't matter. Just your intention. Focus on gifting your energy to her healing."

Flynae feels her body receiving from multiple beings around her. The energy flows like a comforting warmth to her knees. Their help will speed up her recovery time, but she knows what will make it happen even faster.

She stops herself from thinking his name though. His energy is a swirling mix of disturbed emotions. How many of them might be directed at her? The unknown frightens her.

Kovad won't permit her to remain uneasy about something to do with him. *Even if I was upset at you, which I'm not, that wouldn't stop me from responding to you. That might have been reckless. But it was also incredibly brave. How can I help?*

Hold me. Be my catalyst.

He creates the mental landscape of the meadow in their space and takes her to it. Lord Thyde's emotions are intense for a few moments while he works to get them under control.

She holds onto his neck and nuzzles her head against him.

Within a few minutes, she sleeps.

26

E91 I Do (Flynae)

Everything is quiet when Flynae awakes. A glance at the time reveals she slept the day away. Even Kovad is asleep.

On the stand next to her bed are a glass of water and a glass of wine. Her throat is parched; she drains the water at once before picking up the wine.

She swings her legs off the bed and realizes her knees don't hurt.

Panic grips her throat. Her chest tightens making breathing difficult.

What did I do? I was so stupid. She shakes her head in frustration.

Suddenly, the room is too wide and open. Flynae's hands shake, and she almost spills the wine as she sets it down. She rushes across the room, opens the closet, backs into a corner, and closes herself in.

The enclosed space enables her to begin to get her air back. The calmer she grows, the more her thoughts turn to berate herself.

If the Emperor had walked in while I was using Kovad to help me heal. A small sob escapes her. *I can't reveal him. I can't let Seko discover there is anything beyond me.*

Flynae brings her knees up, puts her face against them, and cries. She cries until her eyes and throat burn.

When she's finally quiet, she realizes she's still exhausted. It wasn't as restful to heal without being in Kovad's arms physically. Her mind drifts to a memory of him holding her on Halaa. She imagines her head resting against his bare chest, his skin next to hers.

Flynae sighs.

Remembering the wine now, she quickly gets up, grabs the glass, and returns to the closet. She sips it while going back to thoughts of Kovad. Why hadn't she asked him to kiss her in the energy shield?

Her stomach clenches as awful memories jumble together, fighting for her attention. Eksar's weight on top of her. Or was it Seko? Or Kovad?

All Flynae wanted was for it to be Kovad. Why can't it be Kovad? Why did he have to be so damn honorable? Their opportunities were so few and far between.

She would give herself to him willingly. At first. How long before she panicked? Seconds? Minutes? It was cruel to tease him with thoughts of intimacy. He wouldn't hurt her, and she wouldn't ever be able to make love. Imagining a kiss between them for too long causes her body to tighten in terror.

The vision they saw was an evil trick from somewhere. She can't ever have a willing sexual relationship. Not even with Kovad.

Fresh tears pour down her cheeks.

Flynae empties the wine before laying on her side and rolling into a ball. Eventually, she falls asleep.

A knocking noise wakes her. From how the sound echoes and carries, she thinks someone is standing outside the bedroom door.

Flynae opens the closet a little. She reaches out and connects with the energy outside the room. It's one of the Kaliah women, the dark-haired one.

"Yes?"

"I wanted you to know breakfast has been served."

"Thank you."

"May I bring you anything?"

"No. I'll be out."

As the energy of the Kaliah lessens with distance, Flynae retreats into the closet and shuts the door. Her stomach rolls with hunger at the thought of food. It's been several days since she's eaten. Her last meal had been steak and wine with Kovad. If she never ate again, her last meal would always be with him.

Flynae, where are you?

What do you mean? Of course, he knows where she is. Where does he expect her to be?

Why are you in the dark, baby?

Her throat tightens. Tears begin welling up again. How does he make her so weak with just a single word? *I'm in the closet.*

Kovad's anger and frustration flare up instantaneously. He hates that she's hiding away in need of comfort. He hates Seko. His thoughts pile on top of the other until he pushes them away and focuses on her.

Tell me what to do, he groans. Kovad goes to her mentally and holds her.

Give me a couple of days. I think together we can undo the slave mark or transfer it, but I want to be sure before we try.

Why? What happens if we just try?

Rather than tell him, she energetically pushes against the mark. In response, it shoots tendrils of sharp pain along her nerves. Flynae presses her lips together to stop herself from making a noise. *Something a lot worse than that.*

His mental being tightens around her. *And what are you doing with the time? What will be different in a few days?*

I want to make sure I can push against it without alerting Eksar or Seko. But I don't want to try with your help yet. We need to be more careful. They can't know about the mindlink. If anything physical happens to me, we need to let it heal naturally.

She senses his resistance.

You want me to let you suffer.

This is the only way. We must let our potential remain hidden until we know how to use it.

Why aren't we asking Senice about the slave mark?

The mention of her uncle's name pains her. Flynae doesn't want him to know. She didn't want any of her family to know what was happening.

Give me a couple of days first. Please.

Will you make it a definite timeline? Two days? Forty-eight hours? His tone is soft so that she doesn't think he's pushing.

Flynae realizes there's no telling what horrors the Emperor might have in store for her and when. How much unmolested time would she have? *Seventy-two hours?*

Fine. If you agree to seventy-two and not one more.

Flynae melts into his feelings of care and worry that prompt him to require these terms. *Yes. I do.*

27

E92 Fear (Flynae)

Reluctantly, Flynae leaves her closet. She changes from one bandeau crop top and harem pants to others of different colors. All the rest of her options felt more like lingerie than actual clothes.

When she runs her fingers through her hair to smooth it into place, she makes a mental note to clip her claws as soon as possible. The last time she'd cut them had been about a week ago, and they're starting to be a little longer than she likes. She prefers they not grow beyond where they start curving and narrowing. That's when they lose their resemblance to fingernails.

After a deep breath, she sets her shoulders and walks from the room. Voices chattering direct her where to go.

The harem is much larger than she'd ever imagined. Multiple dead ends lead to more bedrooms. She wanders about, taking her time to reach her destination. Her stomach decided it didn't want food after all and is no longer twinging with hunger.

As she draws closer to the sound of the others, she passes a room where perhaps a dozen women sit with their breakfast plates, watching a show. Having no interest in a reality program about rich people dating and fucking each other, Flynae hurries past having only seen a well-dressed woman on the projection crying about wondering if she is unlovable.

The room after the media room causes her to pause and inspect it further. Within are the only things that could cause her to feel excitement. It's a music room. Inside are all kinds of instruments including a piano, harp, flute, violin, and cello. How did such a place exist inside of hell?

The majority of the chatter comes from the next room. This single space is larger than anywhere else in the harem and holds a long banquet table filled with all manner of food.

Flynae's stomach flips and then clenches within her, rebelling at the sight. So much for feeling hungry earlier.

She doesn't miss the bottles of champagne that sit near a variety of juices. After grabbing a full bottle and a glass flute, she heads back to the music room. She's aware of Kovad's sadness at her choice and his hope that she'll be able to settle down and eat after a few drinks. He resists his instincts to be disapproving or say something, and she's grateful for this.

When she sits behind the piano, she can't help but wish it was the piano Kovad had bought for her. Everything he'd given her is dear to her, and she misses her room aboard The Destroyer.

Flynae pours herself a glass of champagne and drains it in quick order. She pours another. It seems almost silly to have grabbed a glass. If she was going to be a lush, why not just drink from the bottle?

After setting the glass and bottle aside, she begins playing softly. The music is for her; she doesn't want to disturb their show in the adjacent room.

The melody flows and comforts her. The piano holds the

music; her privilege is to set it free. Her fingers dance over the keys effortlessly. She closes her eyes and gets lost.

The sound of a harp joins the piano. Then a violin.

Flynae energetically reaches out and realizes the two Kaliah are playing with her. One by one, the humans walk into the room to listen until the room is filled with everyone Seko's imprisoned within the harem walls. They bring in pillows and sit down on the floor. Gradually, their energy begins to be renewed.

When one song ends, the Kaliah follow Flynae's lead into another. She ignores the champagne sitting on the floor next to her in favor of providing a release for those present. Their pain dissipates in the company of the beauty created by the Kaliah.

The tromp of footsteps in the main hallway outside the apartment causes her heart to begin racing. Suddenly, she realizes why she hadn't eaten breakfast. There's no doubt in her mind they're coming to take her to the Emperor.

She keeps playing.

The doors to the apartment slide open allowing the guards entry. Her ears don't miss the noise though it is several rooms away. The impending trauma causes her gut to painfully twist in anticipation.

Her fingers move on their own as the footsteps come closer and closer. Only when they pause in the doorway does she stop. The other Kaliah cease playing. The room is quiet.

Determined not to let anyone see her fear, she preemptively stands up. Every eye in the room is watching her.

Kovad? She reaches out and finds Lord Thyde is in a meeting with several generals.

He pauses mid-sentence to respond to her. *What's happening, baby?*

I think I need you.

Okay. He doesn't hesitate. Though he speaks aloud to a room far removed from her location, she hears him through his ears. "This meeting is temporarily adjourned. I'll call you all back here later." Without another word, he walks out, leaving the generals in stunned silence, and hurries towards his quarters.

Flynae swallows with great difficulty and then turns around. With her head high, and her shoulders back, she walks to her escorts.

Several women whisper to another near them: "How is she so brave?" "She knows what's going to happen, right?" "This is the most beautiful thing I've seen."

As she walks down the grey hallways, her heartbeat matches the quick pace of Kovad's. Her hands shake. With the construct down, she has no place to hide. With Kovad back in her head, she couldn't get lost in a fantasy about him as she had before. He's her only shelter now.

As the distance between them decreases, the Emperor's presence comes into her awareness.

Don't let him see any weakness, she tells herself. *Give him nothing.*

She keeps walking.

The guard's footsteps echo off the walls. Phantom chains rattle in Flynae's mind. Her wrists ache with the memory.

Her stomach cramps with trepidation.

This is not the time for a meltdown. Her mental self-talk is scolding.

Just two more minutes, Kovad promises.

It feels like a race to her. Will she or Kovad reach their destination first?

She does.

The guards stop before a room. One of them allows the door to scan his retina. It opens.

Before her is the Emperor's hideous, leering face.

When one of the guards moves to take her arm, she walks in of her own volition.

"I have something I've been dying to show you, my dear," Seko says as she stands before him. He gives a motion, and the guards take her arms, bend her over a table, and shackle her wrists to it. In front of her is a one-way mirror showing an empty room.

He's afraid. She takes another inhale to be certain. In the midst of her fear, she determines to acquire as much information as she can during any interaction with the Emperor. *Why is Seko afraid of me?*

The humans leave the room. The Emperor stands behind her and unclasps her top, allowing it to fall to the floor. As his hand snakes forward to grab her breast, Kovad pulls her attention away.

I have you, baby. Be here, with me.

28

E93 Deal (Flynae)

Flynae throws her arms around Kovad's presence in her mind as he leans to pick her up and carry her to their meadow. Her body trembles in his arms. She nuzzles her face into his neck and fills in how delicious he probably smells while he imagines holding her.

Images of past fantasies flash through her mind. It had been a habit to rely on these. As her mind brings pictures of Kovad kissing her front and center for them both to see, her physical ears and cheeks burn with embarrassment.

It's okay, Kovad whispers to her. *There is no need to be ashamed. You were only doing what you needed to. You did nothing wrong.*

She strokes his neck with her fingertips and experiences the shivers that course through his physical body with him.

Kovad sits down on the ground in the meadow and holds her close. To ease her discomfort, he distracts her with images of sunsets, starry skies, and fireworks.

Flynae gazes into his eyes. *Everything here is just memories and fantasy, right?*

He recognizes she wants a specific response. There's a bargaining tone to her thoughts. Without knowing the motive behind the question, he doesn't want to give a definite answer. *Mostly. Why?*

This place is only as real as our ability to focus on the other's thoughts and projections. If one of us chooses not to participate, then it all goes poof. Her mental form jerks as her body responds to a stabbing agony in her core.

Kovad tightens his hold around her, not wanting her to be distracted by what is happening outside her mind.

That sounds like a fair explanation. Why don't you tell me what you want, Flynae? You don't need to dance around it.

She tenses and presses into him, hiding her face. *Because I can't handle it if you reject me.*

Overwhelmed by her deepest need, Flynae shakes with sobs. She's crying in her mind and physically. With her next breath, she smells the Emperor's glee. *Oh, gods. Why can't I keep myself under control,* she scolds herself.

Kovad pulls her chin up so Flynae's looking up at him. *Right here. Be with me right here and nowhere else, okay?*

She nods and refocuses.

It's not a rejection. He pauses, closes his eyes, and sighs. *I would never reject you. That was only a delay, baby. You have no idea how badly I want to smother you with kisses.*

Flynae continues to watch him, knowing he isn't finished.

Every time you thought about me kissing you or even asked me to, I've noticed how your body tenses. It might always scare you or make you nervous. But I don't ever want to be responsible for a negative experience.

When he stops talking, she drops her head. *So not even here?*

What's the full thought, baby? I can't read your mind unless you think it. He squeezes her for encouragement.

Would you kiss me here? In our place?

Kovad's chest tightens into knots as he can't help but remember what is happening. She's asking him for a kiss while the Emperor is raping her. In a momentary lapse of control, he slams his fist into his bedroom wall. The throbbing in his knuckles is worth the slight release. *If that is what you want, then yes.*

Her head turns upward again in surprise. She searches his face to gauge his level of sincerity. *Really?* Her breath catches as her heart beats faster.

Yes.

Flynae feels it this time: her body constricts with fright. *I do. I can't stop my reaction.*

Kovad leans his head towards her.

A tremor of angst washes over her, leaving her cold and shivering. She closes her eyes, terrified that if she sees the kiss coming she won't be able to go through with it. At the same time, she doesn't want him to change his mind.

He kisses her forehead. *Relax, baby.*

He kisses her temple. *I don't ever want to hurt you.*

Kovad kisses between her eyes. The subsequent shiver running through her is one of pleasure. She relaxes just a tiny bit.

He kisses the tip of her nose.

She tips her head back, her body humming with anticipation.

Burning agony in her gut distracts her. Emperor Seko whispers into her ear. She only comprehends the last two words: "Lord Thyde."

Flynae jerks upright, her hand on Kovad's chest, pushing herself away from him. *Why is he talking about you?* She turns around, her attention going back to physical reality.

Without the mental distraction, the torture her body is experiencing assaults and overwhelms her. She stares down at her wrists, raw and bloody from chafing against the restraints. Seko grips her hair, holding her head up to force her to look forward.

There are now people in what had previously been an empty room. From their clothing, they both must be Lords; though they're each missing their pants.

Flynae recognizes Lord Norgan, except his eyes are dark and hollow now. She's never seen the other man with his shoulder-length jet-black hair before.

"I knew his name would get your attention," Seko says in her ear. "Though I can't comprehend why you're in love with your father's murderer." His hips don't break rhythm while he talks and thrusts into her at the same time.

Between the Lords, in the room in front of her, is a young woman. Lord Norgan takes her from behind while the Lord Flynae has no name for is jerking her head up and down on his cock by her hair.

"You can be the first to know Lord Thyde is receiving a promotion today. I'll be speaking with him as soon as I'm done with you."

Flynae tries to focus on Seko's words rather than the ache in her body.

"Lord Julii committed suicide."

Flynae gasps.

"Don't act so surprised." Seko's voice is cold and harsh. "You're the one who broke him."

Crush you! You think you can pass that blame to me? She bites back the words she wants to scream at the Emperor, unwilling to give him the pleasure of her response.

"As you can see, I already have my newest Lord fitting in nicely. Meet Lord Zeresh."

Flynae studied the new Lord's face. While traces of enchantment present around his being, his aura is laced with a cruelty that belongs to him.

"Now, I don't know what is going on between you and your Lord Thyde–," Seko continues.

My Lord Thyde. Flynae can't help but smile.

"—But I will guarantee his rank and safety as long as you don't meddle with my Lords again."

He's bargaining. Gods. What is he afraid of? Her body rushes with a fresh surge of adrenaline. With great difficulty, she responds, keeping her voice calm and level. "You give me your word that Lord Thyde will not be disciplined or harmed?"

Seko's breath is hot on her cheek as he replies. "For as long as you keep your influence from affecting my Lords."

"Deal."

29

E94 Highness (Flynae)

The Emperor finishes moments after finalizing the deal with Flynae. He promptly walks from the room. Two guards come forwards and unshackle her from the table.

Flynae is fatigued and hurting, but she doesn't want to show any weakness. With a great effort, she stands upright, ignoring the fact that she's naked except for the persistent thought poking at the recess of her consciousness.

One of the men puts a cloak over her shoulders. She holds the fabric around her and walks with them back to the harem.

When the door to the foyer opens, she's shocked to see all the women waiting for her return. Several of them sit on the fountain's edge, while the rest stand nearby or lean against a wall. Their eyes widen as she enters.

Flynae walks inside, maintaining her composure. The room's smell is a swirling blend of surprise, awe, adoration, and respect.

Without a word, she walks through the entry room, past all the onlookers, to the bathroom nearest her sleeping quarters.

She locks the door behind her and slides to the floor. Her stomach spasms with great cramping pains. Sobs shake her small frame.

All she wants to do is wash Seko's scent from her. She's made it this far. The last fifteen feet to the shower might as well be a mile.

A knock on the door behind her makes her jerk. From the aura, she knows the dark-haired Kaliah stands on the other side.

"What?" she whispers. *Just leave me alone.*

The reply is quiet and discreet. "Let me help you, Your Highness."

Highness? Flynae scoffs at the term of respect. A member of the strongest bloodline of her people is reduced to a blubbering mess on a bathroom floor. *I don't even deserve my red hair.*

If you don't, no one does, baby, Kovad responds in a soothing thought. *No one comes close to how strong you are.*

The Kaliah taps again. "Please let me in."

Flynae groans, but she sits up, unlocks the door, and scoots away from the front of it.

The Kaliah enters quickly and closes and locks the door behind her. She drops to her knees next to Flynae and helps her stand. "Bath or shower?"

"Shower." Flynae grimaces with the torment of walking. Her insides are still all twisted up.

"What's your name?" she asks the dark-haired Kaliah.

"Xera."

"Thank you, Xera."

Xera grabs a stool on their way and places it where the water spray will hit it before helping Flynae sit down. Then, without having to ask, she washes Flynae's hair.

While her hair doesn't need it often, Flynae always washes it after Eksar or Seko has their way with her. A thorough cleaning is the only way to try to get their scent off her. But, of course, nothing works completely. There is no way not to catch phantom smells for a day or two after. The stench seems to live in her nostrils.

"Are you the next Monarch?" Xera asks in a barely audible voice.

Flynae's shoulders curl forward slightly as her body tightens. She shakes her head and allows her chin to fall onto her collarbone. "No. Why would you ask that?"

"I've never been near someone with such an incredible presence before. You've grown exponentially in strength since I first saw you sixteen months ago. Please forgive me if I've overstepped. You're the first royal I've met." Xera rinses Flynae's thick locks as she talks.

"You don't need to apologize." Flynae doesn't know what else to say.

"May I ask another question?"

Flynae stifles a sigh. "Yes."

"If you are not the next Monarch, do you know who is?"

Flynae can only think of one answer. Every time she tries to puzzle it out, only one name comes back to her. "My brother. Siah."

"Do you know where he is?"

With great difficulty, Flynae does her best to keep her scent neutral. *Everyone is looking for a savior.* Issiah had allowed Seko to do what he wanted in the human world as long as Seko respected the Kaliah rules. How will Siah handle the Emperor after his blatant mistreatment of Flynae and other Kaliahs?

"No."

Xera leaves Flynae to wash and returns in a few minutes with two towels. After shutting off the water, she places a towel around Flynae's shoulders and dries her hair with the other.

Flynae's legs are a little more steady for the journey to her sleeping quarters. Xera walks with her.

From a drawer near the bed, Xera pulls out a hand-held electronic device. "This will allow you to read and listen to music. May I bring you anything? Water? Wine?"

"Both would be wonderful. Thank you."

After the other Kaliah leaves, Flynae dresses and sits on the edge of the bed. She picks up the device and scrolls through her book options. She's surprised and delighted to find a single category offers hundreds, if not thousands, of stories.

Xera returns shortly with her arms full. "I wasn't sure which you preferred," she says as she first holds up and then sets down a bottle of red and a bottle of white. She also brought a wine glass, a water glass, and a carafe of water.

"Wow. Thank you. That is kind of you."

"My pleasure, your highness. I'll let you rest. Please tell me if I can get you anything else." She bows before backing out of the room.

Flynae sighs and rubs her face with her hands. She grabs the bottle of white, figuring that she'll drink it first while it's chilled, the reading device, and the wine glass, and retreats to the closet.

30

E95 Use Me (Flynae)

Flynae reads until long after everyone else went to bed. During that time, she leaves the closet once to have a glass of water and grab the second wine bottle.

The clock says 2:00 am when she sets the reader aside and drags herself out. Since her room is near the Emperor's quarters, she goes to the music room, which lies on the opposite side of the harem.

Flynae sits in the corner and draws her knees up. Not wanting to wake anyone, she creates a small sound-proof energy bubble about her. Her body trembles with dread as she prepares. The pounding of her heart echoes in her head.

Starting small, she uses energy to pick at the slave mark. Tendrils of agony creep through her nerves. She grits her teeth to stay silent and picks again, a little more aggressively this time.

When the pain increases, she can't stop herself from crying out.

Flynae continues for several minutes. Over time, her energy wanes, and the sound barrier begins to lessen. Tears of desperation and frustration flow down her face. The force she'd exerted against the slave mark was minuscule compared to what would be required to make it change. Unfortunately, this also meant the pain would be exponentially worse. She lowers her head against her knees with a sigh.

A hand touches her shoulder. She jerks and looks up to find both Kaliah women sitting before her.

"How can we help?" Xera asks. She nods her head at the blonde Kaliah. "This is Hailen. Tell us what you need us to do."

Flynae's throat tightens. Asking and accepting assistance has never come easy to her. "I need a sound barrier. I can't accurately test the slave mark and maintain one myself."

The Kaliah nod and work together to create a soundproof space around Flynae.

This is the opportunity she's been waiting for. But, as she resolves to use her full efforts against the slave mark, her body tightens and shakes with fear.

She takes a deep breath.

And delays.

She takes another.

With all the effort she can muster, she energetically pushes against the slave mark. Every nerve in her body lights up in anguish as if she's being cut open by millions of little knives.

Flynae screams. The noise bounces off the barrier and assaults her ears, making it sound even louder.

Flynae. Kovad is instantly awake and holding her in their shared mind. He sits up and swings his legs off the edge of his bed. *What's happening, baby?*

She doesn't respond as she fights to regain her breath. Everything hurts. Every movement is a struggle, even expanding her lungs. Sweat pours from her, and she starts shivering.

Kovad waits for her.

The Kaliah wait for her.

Flynae ignores them and stares at the doorway; tears blur her vision. If Eksar was alerted by her efforts, she would see or hear something within seconds.

"Go," she whispers to the Kaliah and weakly makes a waving motion. "You shouldn't be with me if someone comes."

They hesitate.

"Go!"

Xera and Hailen trot from the room, leaving her alone on the floor.

Flynae strains her ears for approaching footsteps. She holds her breath to listen better. Nothing seems out of the ordinary. There is no commotion from the Emperor's quarters. No guards rush in her direction.

She sighs and allows her body to relax. Her thoughts turn to Kovad. *I'm sorry. That was a horrible way to wake you up. I didn't know what would happen.*

He squeezes her as the scream echoes in his memory. *Did you learn anything from this*—he pauses to shudder—*horrible experiment?*

I think so. I think I can attempt to manipulate the slave mark without drawing notice.

What do you plan to do with this information?

Her body tremors renew as her brain resists thinking about the next step. *Practice.*

Kovad sighs and rubs his face with his hands. *Practice? Why do I get the feeling that looks the same as what you were doing tonight?* His frustration and concern turn to rage.

Flynae tenses. Her throat constricts.

I'm not angry at you, baby, he groans. *Just*— He exhales. *Please, tell me the reason you think torturing yourself is a necessity.*

I think we can get rid of it. Or change it. I don't know how yet. But I'll need to be in control of my energy during that time.

Will you let me help you?

She takes a moment to consider. *I think that's safe. If Eksar doesn't know I was tampering with it, then he wouldn't be able to detect you either. Unless he just wants us to think he isn't aware.*

Fresh despair from her last thought overwhelms her, and she begins crying again.

Kovad tightens his mental embrace on her.

The Kaliah tiptoe back in. Xera gently pulls Flynae's head and torso into her lap. Hailen sits against her and runs her hand back and forth over her lower leg.

The comfort flowing from the three of them soothes and relaxes Flynae. She didn't realize she was falling asleep until she feels her body being lifted. Then, with a gasp, her eyes fly open. Xera and Hailen are carrying her.

"Peace, highness. Let us get you to bed," Xera whispers.

Moments later, the Kaliah lay her down and help her to be more comfortable.

"Do you need anything?"

Flynae shakes her head. "Thank you."

Xera and Hailen quietly back out of the room.

The space is immediately too large and open.

Flynae's breath quickens, but she can't move. She's too weak to run and hide.

Breathe, baby. Kovad inhales and exhales slowly for her benefit.

She turns her attention to listening to him. Her tension gradually unwinds, but now she realizes a new problem. *I'm not going to be able to walk tomorrow. How do I cover this up?*

Don't be silly. This is why you have me. Use me.

She hesitates. *Okay, but we can't touch the marks on my wrist. They must remain.* Her thoughts begin to quiet. Listening to his breathing is lulling her to sleep.

How do we manage that?

We start with intention. That should work. Flynae drifts off.

31

E96 You (Flynae)

Flynae opens her eyes and stares at the ceiling, allowing the details of the night before to come back to her. She lifts her arms and finds with relief her wrists still significantly chafed.

A phantom breath from the morning before tickles her ear, and she whimpers with the memory of Seko behind her.

Most of her body strength recovered overnight. Realizing she can move, Flynae races to huddle in the closet.

The reader is still there from the night before. She picks it up and navigates to the music options. Her heart leaps with delight when she discovers she can sign into her music library. Listening to the playlists from Will and Fennec kept her sane during times when she wanted to give up and die. At the top of the list is a new one. According to the tag, Fennec created and shared it with her a month ago.

She taps the screen to display the list of songs and hits play.

The music begins playing from speakers in the bedroom. She cracks the closet door so the sound is pure and not muffled.

From the guitar alone, she's almost sure her brother is the

one playing. When she hears his voice singing for her, she rolls onto her side and allows the tears to flow.

For the next hour, she lies there listening and crying. When Senice sings for two songs, she starts bawling. Her uncle never voluntarily sings, and now he is exclusively for her.

What's happening, baby?

Words abandon her, so she amplifies the music in her mind so Kovad can hear. He holds her for a few moments before needing to continue with his day.

When the playlist ends, she takes a few minutes to compose herself and then gets up and changes her clothes.

Not caring about breakfast, she heads to the bathroom and uses the mirror to braid the sides of her hair back in two rows on each side. Then, she pulls the front back to flow behind her.

Flynae picks up the fingernail clippers and holds her hands over the sink. Her claws arc much longer than she ever allows them to be.

She places the blades near her finger and presses them down through the keratin and grown-out vein. Bright red blood drips into the white basin. She moves on to the next, barely pausing between each one, giving them all the same cruel treatment.

The pain isn't as satisfying as she wanted it to be, even with all ten digits leaking blood into the sink. So now, she's frustrated and has an annoying mess to clean up.

Who did that to you?

Of course, you would check in just now, she thinks to herself with a sigh. *I did.*

Why?

I just– She doesn't have an answer. Then, after a moment, she adds, *It seemed like a good idea at the time.*

Flynae grabs a small towel and holds it between her hands

to stop the bleeding. After a few minutes, she checks her right hand. A few nails still seep blood. *Gods. This is annoying.*

She waits a bit longer and rechecks her right hand. This time it looks clear.

When she pulls the towel away from her left hand, it sticks to two fingers. She rips it away, and they start bleeding again.

Keeping the cloth around her left hand, she retrieves the reader from her room and sits near the window with a view into space to read.

Xera comes and checks on her after a while. "Can I get you anything, your highness?"

Yeah, you can stop calling me that. Flynae tries to banish her moodiness, knowing that the other Kaliah can smell her. "No, thank you. I'm fine."

Xera leaves and returns a minute later with a bottle of wine. When she offers a glass, Flynae accepts it with a smile. Xera sets the bottle on the nearby table before walking away again.

Flynae continues reading the book she found about early Kaliah customs, hoping that at some point it would mention slave marks. Finally, after about an hour, she came upon a reference to an ancient Elvish book. She recalled that her father had owned a leatherbound, handwritten copy. Flynae had only seen the interior text once as a child, but she remembered it was like an Elvish encyclopedia. Her heart leaps into her throat. This could be the book she's looking for.

Kovad! Excitedly, she calls his name much more aggressively than she'd intended.

His response is concern and curiosity. *Yes?*

Remember when you told me to use you?

Yes.

I thought of something.

When she doesn't continue, he prompts her. *Okay?*

Flynae hesitates, reluctant to ask for assistance.

Baby, whatever it is, the answer is yes.

But you haven't even heard my idea.

I don't need to. If you think it's important, then I'll do it.

Her stomach twists into knots. Even thinking about it is difficult. *I need you to help me look up a book. I don't have access to it here.*

Give me thirty minutes, and I can be at my computer.

When he sits at his desk, she shows him how to change his computer's language to Kaliah. The language hid in plain sight under a made-up nonsense name. She assists him in typing the Kaliah words to search for the Elven book. When they find it, she uses his eyes to read.

Kovad's surprised by her reading pace. She only needs to glance at a page for a few moments while her mind captures every detail. Then she moves on to the next while her brain processes the information.

There. It's information about the slave mark. Only the original owner can make a transfer. A slave can't enter into a life pact except with the slaveholder. This dissolves the slave mark, though. The slave must be freed before they can bind their life to anyone else.

Kovad bristles every time she reads the word slave.

Flynae gasps. *Oh, gods, we might have found the answer—Royal blood. Anyone of royal blood with energy control greater than the slaveholder can transfer the mark. So I can transfer the mark.*

Transfer? Who would we transfer it to?

You.

32

E97 Planning (Flynae)

You want me to hold control, ownership over you?

Flynae detects the disgust he's trying to hide concerning the slave mark and knowing all these terms apply to her. *Why not? I trust you. Completely. Implicitly.*

Kovad hesitates, processing the situation and what she's suggesting. While he's worked tirelessly to be worthy of her faith, he can't help but believe he doesn't fully deserve it.

Did you need a more formal request? Flynae tries in vain to stifle a smile while maintaining a mostly serious tone, as she thinks to him, *Lord Kovad Thyde, will you sign your initials on my back and be my slave mark holder?* Her levity is rewarded with a slight chuckle.

If that is your desire, then yes, my lady.

With another detail finalized, fear washes over her. She leans into his presence in her mind. The memory of when the mark was made looms. Transferring it is going to be much more difficult than the original process.

What's your plan for accomplishing this?

Well, I'm still in the preparation stage. I need nightly practice to keep my energy focused through the pain. Flynae shudders momentarily with a fleeting shadow of dread. *I'm certain that Xera and Hailen will assist in keeping the sound contained.*

Kovad breathes through the rage that surges in response to her thoughts. The sounds she needs restrained are her screams. *Let me help. Please. At least let me be present and hold you here.* He exhales and waits for her answer.

Flynae's heart pounds in her throat, trying to stifle her reply. *Are you sure?*

Baby, I would rather go through everything with you than have you endure anything on your own.

His words relax her body and mind. She sinks into him. *Thank you.* Everything is easier when she knows he'll be there.

I only have a few more moments. How much thought have you given to the actual where and how?

Just vague ideas so far. Being ready for any opening. We only need a few minutes. The transfer—her body trembles as she thinks back and considers how long she'd been tied to the pole when Eksar originally marked her—*shouldn't take more than two to three. I'm most unsure about the location. Someplace enclosed and private would be ideal, like a shuttle, but I don't want it traceable back to you.*

I can pull one of my spy ships from The Dominion.

You have spies on the Emperor's flagship?

Of course, I do. I haven't trusted him in twelve years.

Twelve years. His faith in his liege failed the day he touched her.

Do you ever wish you could go back to when you did?

And be one of his mindless drones? Absolutely not. He immediately regrets his hasty remark as he considers how she has paid for his freedom. *I do sometimes wonder whether or not I could have changed the outcome for you.*

Flynae feels his guilt so deeply she can almost smell it. *Kovad.*

Yes, baby. He exhales and pushes most of his emotion away, sensing how much it's affecting her.

I forgive you.

He grips her mental being as tightly as he can, leaving phantom bruises on her sides. His lips press against the top of her head. *I don't know how you're so strong. And amazing.*

She laughs, mostly so she won't cry. *It's just stubbornness. Comes with the bloodline. Call it a family curse.*

Hold on, baby. We're going to get you out. Where no one can touch you without your permission ever again. Let me know what time tonight, and I'll be there.

Flynae shivers as his presence draws away. Though the mindlink doesn't allow them to be truly distant from one another, she craves more of the close times when she can acutely feel his affection for her.

The memory of the last few minutes makes her melt. Her head tingles where he would have kissed her had they been physically together. She recalls the imaginary kisses from the day before. On her forehead. Between her eyes. Her nose.

While she was being raped.

Bliss morphs into fright.

Her body constricts.

She's remiss in insinuating that they could ever be more than they are. How can she ever believe she can be intimate without panicking?

Am I leading him on? Her mind continues her flurry of trepidation.

Flynae. His calm thought cuts through her mayhem.

Yes?

I have no expectations about what you can or will do in the future. Let's focus on getting you safe first. One mountain at a time.

A knock on her bedroom door pulls her back to the present and away from him. Sensing Xera's aura nearby, Flynae gets up to see what she wants.

The dark-haired Kaliah stands there with a glass of red wine and a bowl of tomato bisque soup.

"You haven't been eating, your highness. I was hoping I could encourage that."

Flynae eats in her room and decides afterward she needs to stretch her legs. The harem is equipped with a full gym, but that doesn't sound appealing.

The music settings through the e-reader allow her to play over multiple speaker zones in the apartment. She sets hers for the foyer and begins dancing around the fountain.

One by one, the rest of the women make their way over to stand in a doorway and watch her. She smells their fascination and adoration. Beyond those scents, though, is the smell of peace and contentment that comes from watching something beautiful. Through her act of defiance and escape, Flynae is able to provide moments of relief to those living in the gilded cage with her.

33

E98 Training (Flynae)

By 10 pm, Flynae is anxious to start working on the slave mark practice. The area of the ship near the harem is relatively quiet.

Seko had already stopped by and chosen a girl for the evening. Flynae learned from Xera and Hailen that he never returns to the apartment that day after selecting someone to torment.

Lord Thyde is in his room for the night, and she doesn't want to cut into his sleeping hours.

With a nod from Flynae, the other two Kaliah follow her into the music room and shut the door behind them.

Flynae leans against the wall, her legs suddenly unsteady. Her heart hammers too loudly in her ears and builds to a roar as her mind focuses on nothing else. When Xera touches her arm, she jerks and releases an involuntary cry.

She crumples to the ground and hides her face with her hands while her breath starts coming too quickly. The situation is a nightmare, something straight out of a horror story, where the character is caught in a bear trap and has to chew through their leg to be free.

Just breathe, baby. Kovad draws close to her in their mind and pulls her back against his chest. He inhales and exhales deeply and slowly, his face near her ear. *You're so brave and strong. I know you have this. I'll be here. You're not alone.*

Flynae allows his voice and presence to soothe and comfort her. When she thinks she's ready, Flynae looks up at Xera, who holds a watch. "Okay. Let's do this. Keep track of the cumulative time and pause it if I pause."

"Understood, Your Highness."

The two Kaliah women form the sound bubble around her as Flynae lies down on her side.

Flynae leans into Kovad and permits his energy to contribute and enhance hers. The flow between them is like a circle instead of a singular direction. Neither of them is diminished by it.

After a deep breath, she exerts their full combined force against it. Her body ignites with white-hot fire. Her screams echo back into her ears.

Flynae ignores everything except for the response of the slave mark. She can feel it loosening, like a hard rock melting to putty. This is how it needs to be for Kovad to write his initials over Eksar's. For a long drawn-out moment, she's hopeful.

Then, the pain comes crashing down like a tidal wave. Flynae's head spins and throbs. She loses focus and stops, gasping for breath. Every inhale claws and tears her throat like the air is filled with shards of glass. The side of her head against the floor pounds with a dull ache.

She opens her eyes and finds Xera lying over the top of her. The dark-haired Kaliah sits up as Flynae stills. Tears stream down her face.

"What–?" Flynae's voice is barely a scratchy whisper.

"You were thrashing and hit your head on the floor." Xera

wipes her eyes.

"How long?"

The dark-haired Kaliah consults the watch. "Twelve seconds."

The words sting like a knife to the chest. Her throat constricts.

Twelve seconds.

Twelve seconds that were an eternity.

Flynae nods. "Okay."

She braces herself to resume.

A tear trickles down her cheek. Only that isn't right. Her head is sideways on the floor.

She realizes she felt the tear on Kovad's cheek. He's keeping back most of his emotions, but a tear had snuck through.

Delaying will only allow the fatigue and fear to catch up with her.

Ready? Flynae asks him.

Ready, he replies with a resigned sigh.

She gives the other Kaliah another nod. Hailen takes the watch while Xera leans over Flynae again.

The world around her goes dark while her body lights up with the searing white agony. When she thinks she can't endure for a moment longer, Flynae forces herself to count to eight, a number oft repeated while dancing.

She gasps for air as soon as she withdraws her energy from the mark.

"Twenty seconds, Your Highness." Hailen sounds like a timid yet hopeful cheerleader.

Progress. A tiny bit of progress.

Flynae starts violently shivering. Her sweat-soaked body is rapidly cooling.

Xera turns to Hailen. "Go grab a couple of towels and a blanket."

The blonde nods and rushes away.

Thirty-two seconds. One-sixth of what I need to prepare for. Flynae tries to encourage herself and maintain positive thoughts.

You're doing amazing, baby. Kovad holds her side, allowing her to pretend to feel a bruise forming from his hand. *I'm so proud of you.*

Once Hailen returns, Xera wipes as much sweat as she can from Flynae's head and neck before wrapping the blanket around her.

"Let's go again." Flynae's voice is barely audible.

Lord Thyde groans. She notices him clenching and unclenching his fists as he gets up and paces his room. As soon as she's ready, he recommits to being present with her.

They go again.

And again.

And again.

Each effort is shorter than the last.

Flynae no longer has the energy to speak. She just looks up at Hailen to read off the newest time.

"Five seconds," the blonde murmurs. "But that takes you over a minute. Sixty-one cumulative seconds."

One third. Her mind and body are trying to shut down on her. Even simple math scarcely computes in her head.

Unable to muster the strength to speak, Flynae holds up an index finger. One more.

The other Kaliah exchange worried glances.

Baby, you're barely conscious.

Her body is too tired to sweat anymore. She shivers under

the blanket. Every movement and expansion of her lungs is searing agony.

I'm still awake. One more.

Why do you have to be so stubborn?

We talked about this earlier.

Flynae clings to Kovad's aura in her mind and does one final dig at the slave mark.

The next thing she's aware of is multiple hands grabbing her. Flynae screams and thrashes about. Her feet fall to the floor as two people get a firmer grasp on her upper body.

"It's okay, highness." Xera's soft voice cuts through her confusion. "You passed out. We're getting you to bed."

Flynae relaxes.

Kovad! She tenses, waiting for a response.

I'm still here, baby. You pushed yourself too hard.

Flynae sighs. *It's not enough.* Tears swell up in her closed eyes.

Shh. You did amazing.

I want to be ready. There isn't much time. She gasps with pain as Xera and Hailen set her on her bed. Her body melts into the mattress. *Would you look at Seko's public schedule? What appearances, engagements, are coming up?*

I'll have it for you first thing in the morning, my lady.

Thank you. Her eyes close in exhaustion. *I love you.* Her final thought pushes through as she's too tired to stop it.

After a short delay, he replies, *I know, baby.*

34

E99 Healer (Flynae)

Flynae wakes after two hours of sleep, barely enough time for her body to recover and allow her to move. She rolls off the bed to her hands and knees on the floor and crawls to the closet.

Only when she's inside the dark enclosed space does she realize her heart is racing. For several minutes, she works on breathing and calming down. Thoughts of Kovad come to mind. The connection between them is strong, though he is sleeping. His energy still contributes to the renewing of her body.

Flynae leans back and closes her eyes. Suddenly, she is no longer in the closet on The Dominion but running through a hallway in the ranch on Halaa with a magnum bottle of wine in her hand. She turns a corner and trips. As she falls, Kovad catches her. His arm wraps around her waist, his hand grips the bare skin of her side.

Flynae instinctually melts into him and inhales his care and affection. One moment, she is blissful and allows him to hold her; the next, she pushes him away and yells, "Don't touch me." His eyes lower with sadness as his scent turns to grief.

In the vision, she runs outside and away from him.

Flynae gasps for air as she comes back to the darkness of the closet. The world spins around her. Her throat and lungs constrict making breathing difficult. A hard pit forms in her stomach.

She lays on her side, hugging her knees, and cries.

What did I just do? Why am I hurting him?

The bitter truth creeps into her mind and elevates her current mental and physical agony. How does she ever expect to have an intimate relationship with Kovad? In the tick of a second, her emotional stability can fail. She might believe she wants to kiss him and lay with him, but the most likely reality is she won't ever be able to. If she cares about him, she should let him go. Knowing his past, he probably won't replace her, but she can at least mitigate the pain she causes him.

With her mind made up, Flynae lays there bawling until she falls back asleep.

A female scream from the foyer wakes her.

Flynae sits up, blinking her eyes in the pitch darkness, trying to find her bearings. The decision she made a few hours before returns to her memory, but she pushes it from her thoughts. Any plans concerning it need to be made while Kovad is asleep.

The woman in the other room screams again.

Flynae jumps up and hurries out.

Over the course of the last couple of days, she'd learned all the ladies' names by listening to them talk to each other. She recognizes the thin, naked, brunette writhing in pain on the floor as Rose.

Hailen kneels next to her, surrounded by a few other hovering women as Rose continues to moan and cry out. The blonde Kaliah looks up at Xera. "We need a healer."

Flynae pulls her hair back behind her shoulders and trots over. "I'm here. I'm a healer."

Xera's mouth drops open. "I don't mean to be disrespectful, Your Highness, but you aren't even a century, are you?"

Flynae lets out a single laugh. The sound is light and without judgment, as she understands that most healers can't mend more than a bruise until they're at least a couple of centuries. She probably wouldn't be of much use either if she didn't have the mindlink with Kovad. He strengthens and enhances all her energetic abilities.

"I'll be sixteen next week." She pushes the girls out of her way so she can kneel next to Rose. "What happened to her?" When she gently touches Rose's lower abdomen, Flynae winces at the pain feedback that takes her breath away.

"Seko," Hailen mutters disdainfully.

With a gasp, Flynae says, "I think her pelvis is cracked."

Several ladies exclaim with horror.

The sadness and desperation in the room grow to an overwhelming level, and Flynae struggles to keep her breathing even. *Do not cry,* she scolds and commands herself as her body begins to tremble slightly. *That is an avalanche of emotions you can not deal with now.* Reaching out mentally, she whispers, *Kovad. I need you.*

The commotion around her had already caught his attention. *I'm here, baby. Whatever you need.*

Bethany lets out a sudden shriek. "That's how Mika died. They didn't treat her, and they left her here with us to die like an animal."

At her realization, several other women start to hyperventilate and cause a panicked commotion.

Flynae takes a deep, deliberate inhale before yelling above

the din in a clear, calm voice. "Quiet!"

The room is silent except for the moans from Rose. All eyes turn to Flynae.

Looking at each one in order, she begins giving commands to those who are the most hysterical.

"Bethany, go get hot water."

"Lucia, grab some blankets."

"Graiclynn, a pillow for her head."

"Lily, bring Rose a shot of whiskey."

None of those items were really needed, but Flynae knew it would be helpful to give them a purpose. With their frazzled energies a safer distance away, she begins channeling healing to the compromised bone. She jerks with pain as her body takes on the wound at an other than physical level and lessens the agony for Rose.

A comforting aura envelops her mind, and a flash of white light jumps from her fingertips into the woman below her hands. Kovad's mental embrace flared her abilities.

When the injury is no longer in danger of being made worse by movement, Flynae makes a motion with her head. "Let's get her into bed."

The women swarm to assist. Flynae keeps her hands on Rose's hips as they walk. Moments later, Rose is gingerly set down in her room.

Flynae stays next to her for another minute. She wants to do more, but she needs to be careful not to reveal the extent of what she's capable of with Kovad's help.

Standing up, Flynae reaches out to Jasna. "Stay with her, please."

Jasna nods.

"Come find me if I'm needed. Rose is going to feel bruised

for a few weeks, but she should not be in intense pain."

Jasna's eyes are wide with awe. "Yes." The girl pauses. "Your Highness."

Suppressing a groan, Flynae flees the room for her closet. Her heart hammers and races.

Deep breaths, baby. Kovad is still there, still holding her in their shared space.

She begins to relax and focus on him when her voice from that morning's vision echoes in her head yelling, "Don't touch me!"

Flynae quickly pushes all thoughts, feelings, and images related to it out of her mind.

What was that?

Flynae sighs, wishing he hadn't noticed.

What are you hiding? What are you afraid of? He's trying not to push too much. He doesn't expect her to tell him everything; she's allowed her secrets. But something about this one gives him an uneasy feeling in his gut.

It's—she pauses not wanting to lie and call it nothing—*unimportant.* Those words don't feel like truth, but it's the best answer she can come up with.

Kovad rejects his next thought from being a serious, directed question. *You know you can talk to me about anything?* He believes she knows that and has a good reason for withholding something. Finally, he comprehends why it's bothering him. *Please let me know before it can become as bad as last time.*

Before what does?

You suppressing memories and emotions. Last time it got in the way of helping you. I don't want to discover that during a moment when you need me.

Okay. If it gets in the way, we can discuss it. I promise.

35

E100 Backward (Flynae)

Did you look at Seko's schedule?

Yes. He has a public speech followed by a banquet scheduled in nine days.

Gods. That's not very long. Flynae scrubs her face with her hands.

Lord Thyde is silent and broody for a moment. *You're already pushing yourself so much. And you're not eating.*

Flynae bristles defensively. *I ate*—she takes a minute to think about it—*yesterday.*

That's once in several days. His next thought is quieter. *I can't watch you starve.*

While Flynae understands his concern, she knows Seko and Eksar won't let her die that easily. The last time she had become overly weak from not eating, Eksar kept her restrained in the dark, dirty asylum on Moki and told the doctors to give her intravenous nutrition. The experience was not one she wanted to repeat.

After an involuntary sigh, she replies, *I'll do better.*

He embraces her in their shared space and plants several

kisses on the top of her head before withdrawing.

Feeling a little recovered from the morning, Flynae gets up and decides to at least walk about and graze. So far, she hasn't found a time when there isn't food and drink available in the harem. Meals are served three times a day; between those hours and even overnight, fruit, nuts, meats, and cheeses are always set out.

From what she has seen, the Kaliah are the ones that mostly consume the alcohol. The humans will often have a single drink or glass of wine but refrain from getting intoxicated. Apparently, the Emperor doesn't like his women to be dulled when he wants to torment them.

With a glass of wine in her hand, Flynae stops in to see Rose. The human smiles at her weakly when she enters the room. Jasna is still obediently sitting with the injured girl.

"How are you?" Flynae sets her hand lightly on Rose's hip to check the healing process and is pleased with what she finds.

"I'm alive and in a tolerable amount of pain. Thank you."

"Don't mention it." Flynae walks out as silently as she'd arrived. She spends the afternoon drinking and reading by the window.

Evening arrives all too quickly. All day, her thoughts are filled with dread about the work that needs to be done before she goes to sleep.

Nine days. The number looms over her like an insurmountable obstacle.

She can barely focus on the book in front of her as she keeps checking the time every few minutes. Eventually, the day wears away, and practice time nears.

Her body trembles as she traipses to the music room. Xera and Hailen wait for her. The two Kaliah women share a bottle of scotch by passing it back and forth between them. They'd already brought in a couple of pillows, towels, and blankets in preparation.

Xera takes a swig and offers a drink to Flynae. Not knowing or caring what she's in for, she upends the bottle and consumes a huge swallow before smelling or tasting the liquid.

With a cough and slight grimace, she hands it back. "Gods, that's terrible. How does anyone drink that?"

The other Kaliah politely laugh.

"Acquired taste, I guess." Hailen takes another pull of the light amber liquid.

"I think I'm content with wine for now."

Xera nods at a glass and bottle sitting on the piano bench. "That's why we brought wine for you."

As she pours herself some of the wine, Flynae observes how calm and casual Xera and Hailen are trying to be. Someone observing on the outside might mistake the three Kaliah for a group of friends sitting on pillows on the floor, drinking together, and sharing stories.

Flynae sits up against the wall between the other two and sips her drink. "I have to reach three minutes within nine days."

The other women's eyes widen.

Xera touches Flynae's knee. "That's so soon."

Flynae nods and swallows through the lump in her throat. "It is." She closes her eyes in momentary despair before pushing the negative emotion away. When she looks up, she smiles. "So drink up. We're going to need it."

The three of them pass the scotch bottle a few more times. Flynae takes a couple more tentative sips from the sweet and bitter liquid. Each time she tastes it, she makes a face. They're laughing from nerves and the booze when Kovad comes to

Flynae in her mind.

I seem to be interrupting.

Never. She leans into his presence, holding to him fiercely. *I always want you near.*

After draining her wine glass and setting it out of the way, Flynae says to the other Kaliah, "Okay. Let's do this."

All smiles disappear; they're replaced with resigned faces.

Flynae closes her eyes to lie down, and the room spins around her. When Xera places a hand over hers, she realizes she's violently shaking. All the calming presences near her can't make a dent in the terror she's trying to suppress.

Are you ready? she asks.

Are you ready? he replies. *Maybe you need to rest tonight.*

No way. We have no time.

Kovad pulls her into his arms and strokes her hair. *Yes, baby. I'm as prepared as I can be.*

"Here we go," Flynae warns everyone before she starts digging at the mark. Her body bucks and jerks in response to the searing agony. She attempts to breathe through the misery to maintain her focus for longer. When she tries to count, her mind can't remember what comes after three and gets stuck.

Finally, she needs to stop, unable to channel her energy with the same sharp concentration without a pause.

"Eighteen," Hailen reads off in a low voice.

Flynae runs her fingers against her scalp and pulls on her hair to keep from screaming. "Again," she whispers after hardly a break.

She keeps going at an exhausting pace. Kovad endeavors to slow her down, but she barely hears him.

Three minutes in three minutes, she thinks over and over.

The pain fades to blackness.

Someone lays a blanket over her.

Flynae's eyes fly open, and she struggles to sit up.

"It's okay. Just rest, your highness." Xera gently pushes her shoulders down against the mattress.

Moments later, Flynae is alone in her bed. *I didn't ask how long.*

Fifty-three seconds. His thoughts reveal that he had kept track for himself.

No, she moans, forcing her exhausted body to roll to her side so she can curl into a ball. *I'm going backward.*

You're still worn out from this morning. You did amazing. I'm so proud of you.

Once more, she's unable to hide in her closet. Even in her mind, she's trapped lying in the middle of a great vast space.

Kovad lays down behind her and pulls her mental being up against his.

She immediately feels a little calmer as she notices the lack of distance between them.

Is this spooning? she asks, having only read of the intimate cuddle in a book before.

Yes.

She laughs.

Why is that funny?

Because it's so intimate. We're so intimate. I can't hide or sensor a thought from– Her thought breaks off as her voice from the vision screams, "Don't touch me." Flynae pushes the memory to the back of her mind as she stiffens and leans forward away from him. Apparently, she does know how to keep a secret.

Surprised by the sudden distance, he asks, *Do you want me to go?*

She's helpless to move physically and mentally. Her body

trembles with cold and fear. *No! Please don't.* Tears stream down her face as she's torn between that morning's resolution and needing him with her now.

Kovad leans against her, almost laying over her, sheltering her from anything beyond him.

I'm here, baby. Relax. Breathe.

36

E101 Observant (Flynae)

I*s that you talking to someone in the future?* *Did you see a vision?* Kovad asks.

Flynae doesn't want to respond. She wishes she could unsee and unhear it.

Kovad recognizes she doesn't deny his assumption. He runs through the short list of people she might be yelling at and considers which of them would cause her such anguish if she were to shout at them. *You're yelling at me in your vision, aren't you?*

She flinches and tightens further.

His temper flares when she offers no rebuttal. *What did you see me do?*

Gradually, Flynae realizes he isn't angry at her; he's enraged by some supposed offense against her that he hasn't committed yet.

Flynae, if you saw me hurting you, please tell me so I can do everything in my power to ensure it never happens.

No, no, no. You didn't do anything.

Then why are you so upset, baby? He tightens his mental hold on her aura.

When she continues to not respond, he proceeds to analyze the information he knows. *Are you distraught because you yelled at me?*

Her single sob is enough to tell him he's close.

He sighs in relief. *Baby, I look forward to when you are safe enough that you scream at me for some asinine reason. I will take no permanent offense.*

You want me to yell at you?

I'm aware it will eventually happen. And I'm all right with that. As long as I wasn't being an asshole. Then I will be irate with myself.

His nonchalance regarding the topic surprises her. Nevertheless, the cuddling and talking succeed in calming her. Flynae tries unsuccessfully to stifle a yawn.

Go to sleep, baby. You need to rest.

She reaches up and holds onto his arm wrapped around her shoulders before drifting off.

***

Flynae sleeps through the night without waking. As she comes to, she's amazed to realize she's still in bed and not in the closet. Her body recalls the phantom pressure of his body pressed against hers in their space. The only way she would be more relaxed and rested is if the embrace had been real. Allowing herself a slight indulgence, she makes the mental memory as lifelike and tangible as possible.

After changing her clothes, she walks from the room with the intention of nibbling on some breakfast. If Kovad wants her to eat more, she will make an effort if only to make him happy.

When she approaches the buffet room, she hears footsteps

approaching the harem. The soldiers are bringing back last night's victim.

A hard pit forms in her stomach.

Last night, she was oblivious of who was taken. Just now, she'd walked by the living spaces where the other ladies were socializing. With a glance, she discerns who is missing.

Jasna. Oh no.

Flynae hurries to the foyer as the naked blonde human is thrown to her hands and knees on the floor. One of the human's blue eyes is swollen shut and black and blue.

Flynae plops to the floor next to her and wraps her arms around the girl.

"I'm okay," Jasna replies with a surprisingly calm voice, returning the embrace. "I've had way worse."

Flynae leans back to brush stray stands from the girl's face and survey the damage. The situation obviously wasn't a new one for the human. "How long have you lived here?"

Jasna looks up with her good eye as she thinks. "About eighteen months."

How could anyone survive this nightmare for that long? She blinks back looming tears and cups her hand over the black eye.

Jasna pulls Flynae's hand away. "I'm okay. It'll heal. Plus, the Emperor will probably ignore me for a few weeks now," she adds with a forced laugh. "You're wearing yourself out taking care of everyone else. I don't know what the three of you do in the music room at night, but I perceive it has a purpose. Save your strength."

The human allows Flynae to help her up.

"Thank you for your concern, your highness. I'm going to clean myself up and go to bed."

Flynae stands there despondent as the girl walks away. Rather than eating, she acquires a bottle of wine and sits near the window to read.

"All they did was fuck her." The six words from her fantasy book jump off the screen and slap her in the face. The girl being referenced in the story had been gang raped by an angry mob.

"All they did was fuck her," the prostitute now working in the palace responded so cavalierly to the horrifying event.

Flynae turns off the e-reader, stands up, and walks back to her room. She sets the device on the dresser and retreats to the closet. As she slides down the wall to the floor, tears start pouring down her face.

How does her situation compare to the one in the book? Would someone say that about what Seko and Eksar have done to her?

No. And if someone is ever so callous to say that to or about you, then that will be their last breath. Kovad notices her distress and the circumstances that had caused it. *Not to spoil the story for you, but the whore from the book betrays your favorite character and hooks up with his father.*

How did you know Tyrion is my favorite character?

Because I can feel your burst of excitement when you get to a chapter with his name on it.

You are very observant.

I want to understand you and be cognizant of how to respond to you in ways consistent with your needs.

37

E102 Spades (Flynae

After Kovad's attention, Flynae imagines she's ready to leave the closet again. She scolds herself for how much time she spends hiding. Her memories and current situation wield too much control over her. She resolves to be braver. The first step is living outside her room more.

Flynae raps lightly on Rose's door before peeking her head in.

The human is sitting up in bed reading. She turns her head at the sound. Her eyes sparkle and squint as she smiles and drops the reader to clasp her hands together. "Hey," she calls out in a weak yet cheerful voice.

"Hi. May I come in?"

"Of course. Please." Rose makes a sweeping motion with her hand to beckon the Kaliah in.

Flynae sits down softly on the bed and takes the girl's hand. "How are you feeling?" She watches the human's eyes, recognizing the ocular movements of someone fascinated with the differences in their physical traits.

"Moving stings a little, but the pain isn't unbearable. How

do I ever thank you?" Rose squeezes Flynae's hand.

"Really. It's not necessary."

The girls fall silent. Flynae focuses on contributing calming energy to the human.

Rose's face and body relax. She yawns. "I'm a little bored of reading. Do you want to play cards?"

"Sure. I'll do that."

"Do you know how to play spades?"

"I will if you tell me."

"Have you played hearts?"

"Yes." Hearts was one of Cellyna's favorite card games. Thinking of it is bittersweet and makes her homesick for Halaa and her family. "What do we need?" Flynae asks.

"A deck of cards and something to keep score with."

"And some wine?" Flynae allows a soft giggle.

"Please." Rose playfully groans. "That's the one thing about being injured around here; it's the only time we feel safe indulging."

Flynae's throat tightens and makes breathing difficult. She can't imagine living in the harem for months or years on end, existing only as one of Seko's playthings. "I'll be right back then."

Within a few minutes, she returns with several bottles of wine, a deck of cards, and a pen and paper. Flynae pours them each a drink and hands Rose the cards. "All right, explain the game."

The rules are similar to several other card games Flynae is familiar with. After only a couple of minutes of explanation, the two of them start playing.

They're several hands in, chatting away like old friends, when Rose asks, "Why are you so nice to us?"

Flynae perceives a deeper sentiment to the words than just the surface meaning. "What do you mean? Who is 'us'?"

"The humans." Rose's voice holds more than a touch of bitterness.

"Are Xera and Hailen not nice to you?"

"They treat us like cattle. Their job is to dress or clean us up when the Emperor requires them to. Otherwise, they ignore us."

Flynae parts her lips and exhales. "I'm sorry. Most, and by most, I mean the vast majority, of Kaliah don't have anything to do with humans if they can help it."

Rose stares at her pointedly. "Then why do you? You're obviously more important than they are by the way they defer to you."

"Well. I have an uncle who can't help himself. He's been sneaking me off to meet his human friends since I was a baby. Much to my late father's dismay. So, now, I have several friends who are humans." Her thoughts reflect on her short list of names: Cellyna, Will, Ryen, Carmi, Kovad. When she thinks of Kovad, the edges of her lips lift in a smile.

"And maybe one who is more than a friend?" Rose lifts her eyebrows twice in quick succession after her question.

"Excuse me?" Flynae tilts her head in mock confusion.

"I recognize the signs of someone with a crush. You have a crush on a human." Rose squeals in delight. "Please tell me about him."

"Oh, gods." Flynae scrubs her face. "Okay." Her face and ears burn. "He's the tall, dark, and handsome type."

Rose leans forward. "Yes." Her legs bounce under the covers. "I need details. Have you kissed?"

"No." She exhales and shakes her head, slightly uncomfortable with the conversation.

Rose's jaw drops. "What? Why the hell not?"

"I don't think all the sentiments are mutual."

Rose stares with a furrowed brow. "Wait. We're talking about a human guy, right? What human in his right mind isn't throwing himself at your feet? I mean, you're gorgeous. I'm not into girls, but I would kiss you."

Flynae suppresses a chuckle, not wanting to be rude. "It's complicated."

Rose narrows her eyes. "Is he married?'

"No." She shakes her head emphatically. "I would never go there." With a huff, she takes a moment to think. "He's just...older than me."

"Oooo. Like college-aged?"

Flynae groans and throws her hands up over her face. "Oh, gods. No. Like twice my age." After a brief thought, she adds, "A couple of years more than twice my age."

Rose sucks in a gasp. "Woah. He's not a teacher, is he?"

"No."

The human leans forward. "And you're how old?"

Flynae realizes the girl hadn't been coherent when she'd revealed her age before. "Almost sixteen."

"And he's in his thirties? Dang. He's gotta be hot if you're into him."

"Very. But he's kind to me, and that's why I can't get enough of him."

Rose leans back against the headboard. "I bet you miss him."

After a brief introspection, Flynae replies, "More than I ever thought possible."

Rose exhales. "Girl, we need something stronger than wine."

"I agree. What do you want?" Flynae stands to leave. "But

not whiskey. That's gross."

Rose makes a face. "Yes. I agree. Vodka is easier. Or some top-shelf tequila. That's it. We need lime and tequila."

"Tequila it is. I'll be right back."

Flynae spends the rest of the afternoon playing cards and drinking with Rose. The hours pass pleasantly, and she almost forgets she's trapped in hell. They eat an early dinner together before Flynae retires to her room to rest, needing to be refreshed for the impending work.

When she's alone, she perceives Kovad's thoughts focusing on her. *Did you have something to say?*

I'm wondering what emotions you don't think I reciprocate.

Were you eavesdropping? she teases.

You are as aware as I am that it is almost impossible not to when one of us is thinking or talking about the other.

I am. Yes.

Baby. He pauses, wanting to proceed carefully. *I adore you. I would give up everything for you. Since your present-day tormentor is the Emperor, my current position brings me closer to you. Otherwise, I would not hesitate to abandon my station if doing so would make you safe.*

Flynae sits down on her bed to avoid sinking to the floor. *I don't know what to say.*

You don't have to say anything. I only said what I did because I need you to know you're important to me.

Thank you. She suppresses any other thoughts as her head swims with confusion.

38

E103 Ice Water (Flynae)

Shortly before 10 pm, Flynae walks into the buffet room and begins emptying any bowls and pitchers she can find. She fills them with ice and water from the bar and carries them to the music room.

Xera and Hailen sit in their usual places near the wall by the piano, waiting and drinking. A pile of towels, blankets, and pillows waits next to them.

Flynae sets down the first two containers of ice water. "I think we might need a few more towels." Without further explanation, she strides from the room to acquire more.

Why am I nervous without knowing the purpose behind your project? Kovad examines her silent consciousness for a rationalization.

Because you recognize I'm scaring myself, her mind answers without permission.

Then why are you doing it?

I need to explore all ideas and see if any help. I'm worried about the time constraints. And I'm desperate.

After placing the fifth and sixth containers of ice water, she decides to go back for two more thinking she would rather have too many than not enough.

"What are we doing?" Hailen asks, eyeballing the strange new collection when Flynae finally sits down.

"Trying something new. Pushing harder." Her next inhale tells her the other Kaliah are uneasy. "When I pass out, I want you to pour ice water on my face."

Kovad groans and clenches his fists.

Xera and Hailen stare at her with wide eyes before exchanging worried glances.

"You can't be serious," Xera says with a shudder.

"I am." Flynae nods and leans against the wall as if the argument is settled. She swallows a swig from the whiskey bottle they're sharing and scrunches her face at the taste. Before handing it back, she consumes a second gulp, which burns worse than the first. "I don't get it."

After claiming a towel for a pillow, she lays down and tries to disassociate from her body, hoping that will assist her through the agony better.

Xera and Hailen form the sound barrier around her. Kovad holds her tightly in their space.

Flynae inhales and hesitates. *Would you count for me? Like an eight-count over and over.*

I can do that.

The numbers will help me know time is passing. And I'll be able to listen to your voice.

He presses his head against hers.

Flynae closes her eyes and attacks the slave mark.

Kovad begins counting. Every time she hears him start over at one, she forces herself to take a breath.

The pain is almost in the background of her consciousness

as if she's watching her body burn rather than experiencing it.

Her mind drifts back a few weeks when he surprised her by dancing a tango with her at the banquet. She replays the steps while he counts them out. For a brief moment, everything else fades away as she submerges herself in the memory. His arm around her waist, her hand in his.

The image gradually disappears.

Frigid water assaults her face.

She gasps in surprise, and some of it enters her lungs through her open mouth. She rolls to her side, choking and coughing.

When she has her breath back, Flynae peers up and asks, "Time?"

"Forty-eight seconds." Hailen's eyes sparkle as she squeezes Flynae's hand. "That was incredible."

Flynae smiles back weakly. Her body shivers as her sweat cools.

Xera lays a blanket over her and leans on it to help hold Flynae's body still.

"I can't delay. I need to go again." Without any other warning, she dives back into the searing torment.

Kovad resumes counting.

The dance scene doesn't return. Everything is pitch black this time. She can hear Lord Thyde's voice and feel his presence with hers, but she doesn't have any visual.

The shadows press in, reminding her of the dead box. Her senses fade as a claustrophobic panic takes preeminence. Her heart pounds in her ears, drowning out Kovad's calm, soothing voice.

Every touch with reality vanishes into suffocating darkness. She can't catch a full breath. Her body bucks and twists, but she's trapped, unable to move.

Cold liquid lands on her face, startling her.

Is the room filling with water? Will she drown?

She opens her mouth to scream, but no sound comes out.

Gradually, she becomes mindful of a smooth, round button under her hand. This little switch is the source of her agony, but her reasoning tells her to keep holding it down. Hold it down. For as long as she can. She can't let up no matter how much she wants to.

More cold water runs into her mouth and nose. Flynae's vaguely aware of choking and struggling for air, but she feels so far away from her body.

The only thing that matters is keeping the crushing button pressed. Nothing else is important.

The darkness fades to a swirling iridescent glow. Hundreds of vibrant specks light up and disappear in front of her. Then those gradually subside.

The only perception left is a persistent freezing and scorching sensation. Her insides are on fire while the surface of her skin is excruciatingly cold.

Flynae sinks. Beneath it all is a quiet place where nothing hurts anymore. As she settles into a state of tranquility, someone calls her name from a great distance.

Her hand falls from the button.

The voice beckons to her even more urgently.

Her heart responds with wild fervor.

She pushes through, back to the darkness, back to the agony, back to the cold and burning.

Her body jerks, and she gasps for breath.

The first thing she's cognizant of is Kovad gripping her in their mind as he silently cries into her neck.

Flynae opens her eyes to get her bearings and sees Xera and

Hailen sobbing. *What happened?*

You almost died. Through his physical ears, she hears his hitching breaths. *I felt you fucking dying, Flynae.*

39

E104 Don't Go (Kovad)

Lord Thyde sits on the edge of his bed holding his head in his hands. His body shakes with tears he can't control. They stream down his cheeks. Never has he experienced a heartache this heavy. Nothing in his life ever hurt this much.

The only thing that cuts through the intense grief and torment is his awareness of Flynae observing him. His arms twitch and cramp with a need to physically hold her.

You're extremely upset. Her thought is more a realization than a statement.

Kovad squeezes his eyes shut and sighs in response to her understated remark.

Yes. Despite his best efforts, he's not able to hold her any closer or tighter in their space. His physical fists clench with the necessity to touch her.

You were dying, Flynae. This time was different than before when all of a sudden you just weren't in my head anymore. I didn't know what happened to you or if you were alive or dead.

Kovad grimaces as he remembers the recent horror from

minutes ago that he wishes he could forget. *Just now, I fully understood what was transpiring. The experience was agonizing. Your essence was fading, slipping away from me. I couldn't let you die like that, trapped as a slave in Seko's harem. You deserve so much better.*

When he pauses, Flynae takes one of his hands and presses the back of it to her lips. Her head bows in shared anguish. *I'm sorry. I never expected you to care for me so intensely.*

Why, baby? I make every effort to tell you how amazing you are. Why wouldn't you be dear to me?

Not many humans get with their cats. I'm basically a humanoid feline.

Kovad's jaw drops before he has to suppress a laugh. *No. You aren't a cat.* He lifts his hand to hold her cheek. *When I look at you, I see an elf. A beautiful elf maiden with stunning green eyes.*

She relaxes into him, completely decompressing.

The only time he's ever observed her so limp and vulnerable is when he's held her while she slept. Her current trusting demeanor is a reward to him.

Thank you. She begins drifting off, only mildly aware of her surroundings. Her body alternates between shivering with cold and being too cold to shiver.

Stay with me, baby. He's suddenly worried she could still pass away if she isn't physically taken care of.

I'm here. Her thought is quiet and weak.

"I think her core temperature is too cold," Xera says. "Help me get her in a hot bath."

Flynae cries out as the two Kaliah women lift her. Every muscle in her body is sore from the intense contractions.

Kovad senses Flynae's dull awareness that they're taking off her clothes. He and Flynae always give the other as much privacy as possible when they're bathing or otherwise in a state of partial or full nakedness.

He's torn now between decorum and his inability to allow any distance between them with her in such a fragile condition.

Don't go. Please. She feebly clutches and latches onto him. *I need you to stay.*

Okay. I won't leave.

He senses the hot water flowing over her skin as keenly as if he's in the bath with her.

One of the Kaliah begins softly stroking Flynae, cleaning her body. When Kovad closes his eyes, his hand is the one he sees washing and caressing her flawless marble skin.

Suddenly, his pants are too tight, and his groin aches. Without conscious intention, his body responded to the incredibly sensual feelings and images.

He scolds himself for being inappropriate.

Kovad.

He can almost feel her breath on his face as her voice sounds like she's whispering in his ear. A thrill runs through his body increasing his arousal.

Relax. We both know it's not real. Can we just pretend that you're here? With me? Holding me?

With a deep exhale, he pushes his physical sensations away and draws nearer to her.

Their mental space morphs into a naturally lit, expansive bathroom. Through the open door, he can see the canopy bed they'd made love on in the vision from a week ago.

Flynae's naked body lays between his legs, her bare torso against his in a great bathtub. He runs a washcloth down her arm, up her neck, over her breasts. His fingers ache to find their spot on her side and bruise it.

She's completely relaxed. Her eyes are closed as she relishes every touch.

The image begins to fade, and he realizes she's falling asleep. Kovad wonders if it was imagined or a vision.

Please be alive tomorrow, baby. He feels awful for his selfish prayer. She'd been close to escaping in another way tonight. Too close.

But that wasn't the freedom she truly wants. He knows that. She deserves the long life of a free immortal.

As the intensity of their closeness diminishes with her consciousness, he becomes even more aware of the throbbing in his groin.

With a groan, Kovad gets up and heads to his shower. He strips down and turns the water to freezing cold. As the stream runs over his body, his mind tells him it's warm. A part of him can't let go of the thought of her in the bath with him. Her skin pressed against his.

His cock grows harder still.

He lowers his head and lets the frigid fluid run over it.

Relax. Her phantom voice whispers to him.

Every nerve in his body lights up. He feels her fingers tracing the back of his neck.

"Fuck." He slams his hand against the wall. Every effort to bring his body back into control continues to be futile.

I need you to stay. Her thoughts continue to tease him.

He spreads his arms and leans against the wall as the shower pelts his back. His body is tense and rigid with unfulfilled desire.

"I can't do this," he says through clenched teeth.

His body screams for release. With every passing moment, he is ever more aware that he won't be able to rest without it.

Sleep is non-negotiable. He needs to be strong for her tomorrow, which means this present weakness must be dealt with.

After tonight's trauma, he's ready to be done fighting. Fatigue is rapidly settling into his body.

He wraps his fist around his erection and closes his eyes.

Kovad.

He can't get the idea that she is there with him out of his head. Her breath against his face and neck. The softness of her skin. The pressure of her body against his.

He quickens his strokes.

The image of her in the green dress from the vision rises in his awareness. He watches himself slowly strip it from her body, revealing every inch of her glorious flesh.

His breath comes faster. The tension and pleasure in his body build until they spill over and release.

"Fuck." He pounds his fist against the shower tile again. His body might be relaxed, but his mind is condemning. Not only did he desecrate thoughts of someone he reveres, but she's only fifteen.

Sleep might not be coming tonight anyway.

Kovad towels off, steps into cotton pants, and lays down in bed. For a little while, he stares at the ceiling. Eventually, he begins to drift off. He's nearly asleep when he hears her scream, *Don't touch me.*

40

E105 Nightmares (Flynae)

"Shhhh." The ice beneath her blades whispers to her. "Shhhh."

Flynae spins around, and Will grabs her hand. After his quick turn, they skate backward together. He moves in close and puts his right arm around her waist. Her left hand lifts to his shoulder. Their free hands clasp. She swings her leg around as she faces him and then kicks off. Almost effortlessly, Will launches her into the air.

Flynae rotates three and a half times before landing gracefully on a single foot, her arms out wide slightly above shoulder height.

Everything except for her and the ice disappears: Will, the arena, the stands. Confused, she circles and finds nothing but ice for miles. She's in a tundra wasteland with no barriers from the wind. The cold cuts painfully, and she begins shivering.

With no idea what direction to go, she starts making a straight line hoping to find something or someone.

Someone. The word echoes in her mind. Someone is waiting for her. Or wanting her. She needs to find him.

A great cracking noise sends her heart into her throat. The next moment, she falls through the ice. The chill makes her gasp, allowing freezing water to flood her lungs.

Flynae kicks her way to the surface. When she tries to grab the edge of the ice to pull herself up, it chips away in her hands, and she goes back under.

The cold is unbearable. The next time her head breaks free, she gasps and screams.

Maybe he'll hear me. Her mind finally supplies her with a name. *Kovad! Please help me!*

Once again, her head sinks under the water. When she comes up a third time, she glimpses his hand reaching out. Her heart flutters.

I love you, Flynae thinks as she grasps him.

The air is cold on her skin as he lifts her out and pulls her next to him. With no strength left, she collapses into his arms. For only a moment, her body relaxes into his.

Suddenly, she thrashes and pushes him away, screaming, "Don't touch me."

Leaving him sad and hurting, she begins running. Before she gets far, she falls and finds herself on her back.

Kovad leans over her. She frantically claws at him, leaving a nasty, bleeding scratch across his cheek. Eventually, he grabs her wrists and restrains her while she continues to shriek.

With a sudden inhale, Flynae starts awake. In vain, she struggles to move. A quick glance at the clock tells her she hasn't been asleep for much more than an hour. Air comes and goes too quickly as she thrashes in the bed needing to get to the closet.

She senses Kovad's eyes fly open. He'd been near sleep but not all the way unconscious.

In no time at all, he understands what's happened and holds her in their space. *Breathe, Flynae. You had a nightmare. None of it was real.*

Except most of it had been real. The memory of the ice water choking her lungs and burning her throat followed by the heat of the bath water.

His recollection replaces images of her bathing with the cold shower he'd taken after. Before he can stop them, remembrances of masturbating flood his mind.

The room is too wide and open as well as claustrophobia-inducing at the same time.

"No. I can't," she whimpers and uses all her energy to slide off the bed.

With no strength to brace her fall, she lands with a bang on her side and cries out on impact. The room spins. Sobs choke her and stop her from getting a full breath.

Baby, please, calm down and breathe.

She senses Kovad sitting up at the edge of his bed and holding his head in his hands.

I'm sorry, he adds. His being exudes guilt.

A place to hide takes precedence over responding. Control and rational thoughts are elusive until then.

After multiple considerations and attempts to get her arms to lift her torso, she realizes the closet is too far away. The space between the bed and the floor is tall enough that she can roll under. She's still not as confined as she'd like, but there are no other options.

Kovad. Even her thoughts are weak and quiet.

I'm here, baby. He squeezes her, and she melts into him.

Don't touch me! The haunting voice of her future self sounds in her head.

Flynae clamps her hands over her ears as if that will drown out the noise. *No,* she moans. *Just stop.*

Why is this still bothering you? Desperation fills his voice. *What aren't you telling me?*

I can't. I can't.

What can't you talk to me about? What did I do? His heart races as his concern and distress grow.

It's not you. She moves her hands up and pushes them against her head as if to remove some pressure.

I can't. I can't. The thought repeats in her mind.

All right. He takes a deep inhale. *It's okay, baby.* He exhales for four seconds. *Calm down. You need rest. Breathe.* While continuing to respirate slowly, he wraps his arms around her as he had at the ranch on Halaa when she panicked from her vision. One arm lays across her collarbone and grips her upper arm; the other is around her waist, squeezing her side.

Finally, she begins to relax as she listens to him.

Her fearful trembles turn to shivers. The metal floor is cold through the thin clothing she's wearing.

Fuck, he groans to himself, desiring to be able to envelop her in a blanket and physically hold her.

Kovad.

Lord Thyde realizes he'd never understood the general obsession with someone saying your name until he heard Flynae say his. Now, he craves her voice like an addict demanding a fix. *Yes, baby?*

I need you. Her thoughts reveal she achieved her intention of directing him back to her instead of the anguish he was feeling. *Can we....*

Even though she can't bring herself to think the end to her sentence, her mind shows him an image of her wish.

What he observes makes him smile. *Yes, baby. I'll spoon you.*

41

E106 Rose (Flynae)

Flynae wakes up a couple of hours later overwhelmed by two sensations simultaneously. The first is debilitating shivers from sleeping on the floor. Her body is still sore and achy from the night before, and the cold aggravates it.

The second is a tight pain in her throat. Drawing her legs up, she grips them for comfort as a deep guilt washes over her. How can she continue to be so selfish when she knows she will eventually push him away? If she carries on, she'll only be making it worse for him.

Flynae chokes back the sobs that threaten to incapacitate her. Right now, her body demands she focus on getting warm. A blanket doesn't sound like it will do the job. A hot shower is in order.

With difficulty, she crawls out from under the bed. She manages to push herself up to her knees but then needs to lean on the mattress to assist her to her feet.

Slowly, she begins walking to the door but pauses after a couple of steps and listens. Silence. When she moves forward again, she pauses as the footsteps she'd heard before continue.

They stop when she stops.

Oh gods, she whimpers.

Kaliah footfalls are typically silent, only detectable to Kaliah if they're actively seeking to notice them. In her diminished capacity, her feet patter across the floor making a noise like a human.

After a hard swallow, Flynae continues to the door. The nearest bathroom door isn't more than two hundred feet away. She takes a deep breath and rushes to it, unable to move faster than a trot.

The noise of her treads echoing off the walls alarms her like someone is chasing her.

Finally, she reaches the bathroom, locks the door behind her, and slides down to the floor. Her heart beats against her ribcage in fright. She inhales air in big gulps trying to consume enough to calm down.

Cold sweat breaks out over her skin, increasing her need to get warm.

She pushes herself up and turns the automatic light switch off. Even though no one else is in the room with her and Kovad is sleeping, she's awkward about being naked in a lit room.

Without any light source, she can't see. Her other senses are reduced in her weakened state so she runs her hand along the wall for direction.

On her way to the shower, she grabs a towel and a hair tie. She hangs the towel on a nearby rod and pulls her hair up on top of her head to keep it mostly dry. Then she strips down and huddles on the floor under a hot stream of water.

When she's finally warm, she turns off the water, wraps the towel around herself, and pads her way back. Her footfalls haunt her ears on the return trip.

The rest of the harem is quiet and sleeping in the early morning hour.

Once she's back in her room, Flynae dresses and settles in the closet with several blankets, pillows, and her reader. She doesn't read for long. The lack of sleep catches up with her, and she shortly dozes off.

Upon arising for the second time that morning, she's relieved that her footfalls have returned to mostly inaudible. From beyond her room, she can hear the quiet chatter of the other ladies up and about as well as the low drone of the television.

With a resigned sigh, she determines to eat something for breakfast. The nightly training makes it difficult to eat anything after midafternoon. She's also hungrier in the mornings as her body craves anything to help it replenish.

On her way to the buffet room, Flynae decides to check on Rose and ask if she can bring the girl anything. Within a day or two, the human should be well enough to be up and walk on her own.

Flynae raps her knuckles on the door and listens. She can't detect any noise from within. Normally, she would at least hear someone inside breathing.

"Rose?" Flynae knocks again but only waits a second or two before entering.

The room is empty. The bed is made.

Flynae's gut clenches. Something is horribly wrong.

She continues further into the heart of the harem and stands in the doorway to the media room.

"Where is Rose?"

Every head in the room turns from the television. Most of them meet her eyes with dull, downturned expressions. Jasna's shoulders slump as she stares at the floor.

"No." The word comes out in a breathy whisper. Flynae covers her hand with her mouth to stifle threatening outcries. "He didn't."

As her grief builds, more and more heads drop their gaze to the floor.

Flynae continues walking, glancing in each room for Rose, knowing that she won't find the girl. She reaches out energetically, searching the ship for Rose's aura. As she completes her circle of the harem, she pinpoints the human's weak life source. Her inability to reach her is maddening.

Flynae sits down on the edge of the fountain and stares at the double metal doors that lead out to the rest of the ship.

Minutes pass agonizingly slow.

Unseen eyes make her skin tingle. She looks up into the invisible camera, knowing its exact location by the sensation on her body.

Rose's life flickers, and then goes out.

Flynae bends over and gasps, holding her stomach like someone punched her.

"No!" she screams, jumping up and running to the doors.

The metal shudders as she hammers her fists against them.

"Seko! You fucking coward!" she shrieks with the full force of her lungs. "I will end you! I will fucking kill you!"

Only vaguely is she aware of the other women and Kaliah entering the foyer and watching her.

"You can't hide behind your guards forever! You reek of fear! Every day your terror grows! Your reign is coming to an end! My eyes will be the last fucking thing you ever see!"

Flynae falls to the floor, exhausted by her outburst and overcome with grief. Tears flow down her face. Sobs rack her frame.

A tidal wave of pain floods over her. She's crushed and helpless beneath the tsunami of emotions flowing from the humans in response to her tears.

"Get them out of here," Xera yells, her voice cracking with unrestrained emotion.

To Flynae's ears, the Kaliah sounds far away.

Someone grabs Flynae's arm and pulls her to her feet. Barely able to walk on her own, Flynae leans on the being guiding her to her room.

When she's deposited on her bed, Flynae turns to see Xera's tear-streaked face.

"This is exactly why we don't get attached to the humans. Their time in this nightmare is much shorter than ours."

After the brief scolding, Xera leaves Flynae alone.

42

E107 Xera (Flynae)

An hour passes before Flynae is in control of herself enough to leave her room. During that time, her emotions oscillate between grief and anger. Now, she needs to vent them with music.

She gets up, walks to the instrument room, and sits behind the piano. Her hands are bruised from banging on the doors, and it hurts to spread her fingers, but she doesn't let the pain impede her.

One by one, the other girls meander into the room and settle on pillows around her. For the next several hours, Flynae doesn't stop playing. Sometimes, she sings; but mostly, she lets the music do the work.

The tunes are all melancholy with themes of heartache and loss. Within only a few minutes, no eye in the room is dry. Even Xera and Hailen are touched by the atmosphere of sorrow and release Flynae creates.

While she plays, Flynae can't help but think about what Rose said regarding the Kaliah not caring for the humans. Obviously, the Emperor succeeded in creating a place of indifference.

Kaliah might not associate with humans if given a choice, but they still hold all life valuable.

Kovad observes how distressed Flynae is at the loss of someone she barely knew and marvels at her capacity for caring.

His attention diverts her focus from losing Rose to losing him. Every day they spend apart is another one gone from his limited number. An imagined metronome ticks off seconds. The pace speeds up as her heart races with turmoil. Each beat is a crushing loss.

Doubt and uncertainty inundate her exhausted psyche. What place does she have in his life? What does her broken spirit have to offer anyone?

Baby, I understand you're hurting, but that doesn't mean you need to question everything. Especially when it comes to you and me.

I hate being apart from you. I could handle everything else if I could just see you at the end of the day. What if I'm too clingy?

Lord Thyde laughs softly. *Baby, we spent ten years unable to have a moment of respite from each other in our minds. I would love to be able to reach out and touch you whenever I'm thinking to you. I'm not worried in the slightest.*

Embracing his confidence helps her be more at ease. She begins playing songs that remind her of him. Almost immediately, the mood in the room lifts.

Footsteps sound from the hallway. She counts twelve guards marching in their direction. Tension builds in her gut. The Emperor's torments are never-ending. What horror does he have in store for them now?

The time is barely mid-afternoon. It's typically later in the day when he sends his soldiers to collect someone.

Moments later, they file into the room. The company is composed of twelve humans holding stun guns and two Kalaih armed with lifeswords on their belts.

Flynae stops playing and sets her hands in her lap as they enter.

The women gasp and back up against the walls.

Two humans march over and stand behind Flynae. When she slowly stands up, one of them grabs her shoulder and presses the slave mark.

She falls to the floor with a cry, and the soldier follows her down without letting up pressure.

Through a fog of agony, Flynae's aware of a pair of guards taking hold of Xera's arms and leading her from the room. Xera is out of sight when the soldiers securing Flynae relent and leave with the rest.

The room is full of chatter. Flynae can only make out fragments as she tries to catch her breath, but the smell permeating the area is surprise.

Hailen helps Flynae sit up and lean against the wall.

"Why is everyone so stunned?" Flynae asks the other Kaliah.

Hailen swallows hard before replying. "The Emperor hasn't taken Xera or me for over ten years now." She pauses to take a deep breath. "He mostly uses us to keep the women in here in line and to prepare a girl if he wants them for something specific."

Flynae turns from Hailen's copper eyes to the empty doorway. "He took her because of me. First, Jasna. Then Rose. Now Xera. They're all people who interacted with me."

Every eye pivots to her. Scents of mistrust, gloom, and despair waft from the collective.

While the event was shocking, Flynae believes she should

have expected this. She's locked in a battle of wills as Seko tries to break her. Failure is not an option, but she can do her utmost to protect those left.

With difficulty, she gets to her feet, rejecting Hailen's attempts to assist. Her footsteps fall heavily as she pads back to her room. The best way to protect the other women is to not interact with them.

Flynae retreats to her closet, leaving the door cracked, and turns on music. For the next few hours, she listens to the songs Fennec and Senice recorded for her on repeat. To her delight, one new song from each of them appeared on the playlist since the last time she'd looked at it.

43

E108 Burden (Flynae)

Flynae doesn't leave her room until all the other ladies retire for the night. Only then does she meander out to retrieve water and wine.

Worries about how to train plague her. She can't ask Hailen for assistance which means she's physically on her own.

At this point, she isn't concerned if Seko hears her. With all the cameras in the harem, he must realize she is doing something. How much of her actions he understands is unknown.

What does worry her is the trauma she can cause the other ladies if she can't maintain a sound barrier. This thought brings to her attention the impact of the training on Kovad. He doesn't get the benefit of being sheltered from her screams, though he did volunteer to assist rather than retreat. If he wanted to, he could pull away and lessen how loud they are in his mind.

After grabbing a bottle of wine, Flynae collects a bottle of tequila as well. Wine isn't a strong enough drink after the day's events. While she's in the buffet room, she picks up a bowl of nuts to take back with her. Eating before training isn't a good idea, but she doesn't plan on coming out again until the same time tomorrow night. Everyone else will be safer if she remains secluded.

As she settles down in her closet to get ready and takes a large swig of tequila, she experiences Lord Thyde's worry.

Baby, promise me you won't push as hard. No one is present to help you, and you almost died last night. None of this means anything if you aren't alive to complete the transfer.

Flynae drops her head into her hands, torn between reason and resolve. His choice of words brings her a little comfort. Rather than say attempt or try, he said complete, showing his confidence in her.

Seven days. The number looms like an unscalable cliff. Failure means the end. No more chances.

We're both dead if we're unsuccessful, she says.

I understand and accept the risks.

A hard lump forms in her throat. He's willing to put his life on the line with her.

She sighs. *Yes. I promise.*

Flynae lays down on the little bed she's made on the closet floor. The bottom layer is a blanket topped with a towel. She covers herself with a second towel and another blanket.

Ready? she asks as she leans into his presence.

Ready, baby.

***

Sleep is filled with more nightmares. When Flynae wakes up, she doesn't remember anything except the sound of Rose screaming.

Her body isn't as sore and exhausted as it was the day before. The promise held, but the lack of progress is disconcerting.

She spends the morning reading, listening to music, and stretching.

As the hours pass, she grows more and more concerned for Xera. Will she be brought back? Eventually, Flynae is too nervous to do more than sit and wait. Her stomach is in painful knots. She wants to reach out and find Xera's life aura but is afraid of what she will find. If Seko kills her, every Kaliah on the ship will experience the loss. How are any of them okay with this?

The helplessness is maddening.

So much of what Seko is doing would not have been allowed just twelve years ago. No wonder he arranged for her father's death. Issiah kept Seko reigned in for several millennia.

What she witnessed in the repurposed sanitarium on Moki plagues her. Eksar is committing nefarious crimes against Kaliah under Seko's orders. But to what purpose?

Her people never used to allow cruelty which means some are under Seko's enchantment. Can she be a counterweight? At least until Siah is found?

The burden weighs upon her like a giant crushing boulder. She's not up against another Kaliah like Eksar. She's up against an elf. What chance does she stand?

Her win over Seko concerning first Lord Thyde and then the other Lords brings her a glimmer of hope. The Emperor hasn't won every round. In fact, his only victories happen when it is just the two of them. Every time someone else is involved, she comes out ahead.

Except for Rose and Xera. She has two intense casualties.

Flynae tucks herself into the confinement of the closet and pulls a blanket over her head. Within her, the child cowers while the warrior scolds her. The warrior desires to win no matter the cost; the child begs to be loved and taken care of.

A heavy ripple in the energy field crashes into her, and she understands Xera is gone.

44

E109 Jasna (Flynae)

The day passes, and Flynae doesn't move from under the blanket in the closet. She's still there when Kovad draws close at the normal evening training time. What he finds in her mind surprises him.

Flynae's warrior self sits proudly with the sides of her hair pulled back in braids. She wears a long green dress with her lifesword buckled around her waist. Her eyes narrow and her jaw tightens as he approaches, but she doesn't turn to look at him. Red glints from the corner of her eyes. In her lap, her hands alternate between twisting together and clenching into fists.

Behind the warrior, the child lays in a ball on the floor, crying. Images of faces cycle through her awareness. Issiah. Lord Julii. Rose. Xera. Issiah. Lord Julli. Rose. Xera. Issiah. Each one signifies a colossal weight of guilt. She feels responsible for their deaths.

Lord Thyde wishes he could encourage the warrior spirit. Flynae definitely needs that part of herself in order to continue to survive, but he recognizes an unwavering persona when he sees one. The warrior wants to fight and kill something. If he engages her, she'll most likely behave in a way she'll regret later.

The blame the child places on herself hurts his heart. None of those deaths were her fault.

Kovad takes a couple steps closer to the child. She visibly quakes as the sound of his footsteps echoes loudly. The image of him stalking toward her father appears clearly before her.

The only word that comes to mind to say as he gathers the child into his arms is, *Baby.*

The two halves come together, and the Flynae he holds is more like a breathing doll than a being. Her eyes are dull. Her mind is empty. Despair pours from her in waves.

Flynae. He gently shakes her.

I can't do it. She buries her face in her hands.

Can't do what?

Any of it. I'm just going to lay here and not move.

While he comprehends her desire, he isn't worried about her making good on it, especially after seeing her warrior spirit ready to tear someone apart. He understands she's depressed and in need of some comfort.

That's fine for tonight. He resists the urge to talk about tomorrow but his thoughts reveal his strong proclivity that she leave her room during waking hours the next day.

No. I won't. I can't be responsible for any more deaths.

You haven't caused any fatalities. Every lost life that you're mourning points back to the Emperor. And you can't hide in a closet all day. Solitary confinement leads to a whole host of psychological issues.

Like anxiety, depression, nightmares, hopelessness? Because I don't deal with any of those already.

Accepting her snarky tone as a good sign, he smiles and squeezes her. *Which is why we can't let any of those grow worse by you secluding yourself. Don't you think that is what Seko wants?*

She exhales hard at the mention of the Emperor's name but considers Kovad's point.

Are you ready to start? he asks.

No. She sinks back down into her earlier feelings of despair. *I'm not–I can't do it anymore.*

Lord Thyde considers allowing her to take a night off but decides to push her instead, hoping that reminding her of her goal will help improve her mood. *Well, then I guess you leave me with no choice but to bring you your lifesword and fight our way out together.*

She studies him for signs of bluffing and finds none. *You're talking about a suicide mission.*

You're taking away our alternative.

Flynae shoves away from him and senses her eyes flaring red at the suppressed mirth on his expression. *You're manipulating me.*

His head inclines slightly. *Yes. If that's what it takes to fire you up again.*

How dare you! She tries to keep her demeanor stern and serious, but she melts into appreciation. Her mind betrays her by whispering, *I love you.*

Someone knocks on her bedroom door, and she jerks and gasps in alarm, having been fully engrossed in being present with Kovad. When she realizes it's Jasna, Flynae groans and wishes the girl would leave her alone. This was the one human left the Emperor could use to strike a crippling blow with.

"Hello," Jasna's sweet, soft voice calls into the room as she apparently didn't wait to be let in.

Flynae hears the girl's footsteps as Jasna walks over to the bed and then to the closet.

The door slides back a few inches.

"I should have guessed the closet first," Jasna whispers.

"What are you doing here?" Flynae pulls the blanket down and looks up at the human.

"Oo. I love the eye shine. Though it does make me a little jealous that I can't see in the dark." She cracks the closet open a little wider. "Scoot over."

"What are you doing?" Flynae repeats. "You shouldn't be here."

Jasna ignores her, slips inside the closet, and pulls it closed behind her. She lays down right up against Flynae and puts an arm over her. "You were in your room all day. I was worried about you. I'm sorry I didn't check on you sooner."

"I'm trying not to get anyone else killed."

Jasna snorts a little as she exhales. "You didn't cause anyone to be killed. Don't be silly."

"You're seriously going to tell me it's not my fault Rose and Xera died?" Both guilt and anger fill her voice.

"Of course I am. We're all ticking time bombs in here. Besides Xera and Hailen, I've been here the longest. Every few months, the Emperor gets bored or something and purges a few girls to make room for some new ones. I've seen it happen several times now. There's no rhyme or reason to it. I suppose I'll be one of the next to go, but you can't take responsibility for his crimes."

Flynae blinks back the tears threatening to choke her, but she doesn't want to cry with Jasna present.

"Oof. You Kaliah have such heavy emotions when you allow yourselves to feel them." Jasna sniffs. "Why aren't you doing the thing you've been doing at night with Xera and Hailen?"

"Because I was giving up."

The words sound stupid to her ears as they come out.

"I don't believe that. You're a warrior. Fight is written all over your face and demeanor."

When Flynae doesn't respond, Jasna continues. "So how can I help? I know I can't do any of the cool shit you Kaliah can, but may I at least be here with you while you do it so you aren't alone?"

Kovad. Do you still want to train tonight?

Yes, baby.

"Alright. Let's do this," she says to both of them.

45

E110 Breakfast (Flynae)

Flynae sleeps the entire night and wakes up to find Jasna still cuddling her.

"Hey, you're awake?" the human says softly when Flynae stirs. "How are you feeling? Last night was pretty intense."

Grateful as always for Kovad's ability to help her regenerate, or her capacity to use him, she hasn't figured out which it actually is, Flynae smiles a little. "All things considered, I think I'm okay."

"Good." Jasna squeezes her before sitting up and opening the closet. "Because I'm famished. I'm a breakfast person and need food right away in the morning. Come eat with me?"

Flynae hesitates.

"Or have a mimosa while I stuff my face. Either way, you're getting up." Jasna grabs her hand and pulls as she stands up.

Flynae slowly relents. *Why does it feel like you put her up to this?*

I would like to say I hold that power. However, I fully approve of this girl.

Of course, you do.

Jasna doesn't release Flynae until they're standing inside the buffet room. When the human squeals, Flynae starts.

"We have waffles today! Do you like waffles?"

"Umm. Not really."

"What is there not to love about waffles?" The girl plops a thick honeycombed breakfast cake on her plate and begins drowning it in maple syrup. "They're light and fluffy. Soft on the inside. A little crunch on the outside if they're cooked right. And a sugar rush to last until afternoon nap."

Flynae downs a flute of champagne before facing the food. As politely as she can, she replies, "Everything you just mentioned. That's what I don't prefer about waffles."

"Oh yeah. You're a carnivore, aren't you?"

"Mostly. If given the option."

Jasna stares expectantly while Flynae hesitates to approach the table. "I'm not moving until you're holding food. Then you can drink all the champagne you want."

With a resigned sigh, Flynae puts a few sausages on a plate.

Jasna frowns with obvious disapproval. "I think a robin eats more than that before sunrise each morning." She signs and smiles. "Better than nothing, though." She grabs a mimosa and begins walking from the room after making sure Flynae follows. "Let's see, shall we eat in the music room? You seem to avoid the media room. Why?"

They sit down on the couch across from the piano.

"I don't like watching shows. I never know what I might see. And once I've seen something, I can't unsee it."

Jasna's eyes widen, and she hurries to chew and swallow a huge bite. "Yes! I was little and watched a horror movie I wasn't supposed to about this clown that kidnapped kids. And then one of the kids grows up and slits his wrists in the bathtub and writes in blood on the wall. I had nightmares for years after that. And I still prefer showers over baths."

"Yeah, that sounds awful. No, thank you." Flynae constricts at the thought of being voluntarily scared.

"What happened to your parents?" Jasna cuts off a chunk of the cake and swirls it through the sticky sap to scoop up as much as possible.

Flynae blinks, caught off guard by the sudden change in subject. "Excuse me?"

"Most of us are orphans, runaways, or 'troubled'." She holds up her first two fingers of one hand with the last word.

"Umm. My mother died delivering me. The midwife had to cut her open to save my younger sister." She struggles to swallow the tension in her throat. "And the Emperor arranged for my father's death a decade ago. He's been planning for me to be here for a while now."

"That's awful." Jasna's voice is muffled by the giant bite she shoved in her mouth while Flynae was talking.

Flynae tries to control the quaking in her jaw as she watches the human and realizes how much she cares for the girl she met only a week ago. Her heart sinks. When she leaves here in six days, it will be the last time she sees Jasna. Tears well in her eyes at the realization.

If she lives the lifespan of an average Kaliah, she will lose so many humans.

To deflect, she says, "So what about yours? What happened to your parents?

"I ran away." Jasna waves her fork about casually.

Flynae smells the girl's regret. "Tell me."

"Well," Jasna rolls her eyes, "there was this guy. He was

so hypnotic. I could just get lost in his eyes forever. He kept showing up at my school at cheerleading practice. Every time we locked eyes, I lost all control and messed up."

Jasna nervously laughs. "I almost got kicked off the team I was such a disaster." Her eyes drift off. "Then, one day, he asked me to run away with him. I didn't have an unhappy home life. I didn't have a reason to leave. But I went."

Jasna blinks a few times before meeting Flynae's eyes. "He and I made out at a hotel room that night. I blacked up. When I woke up, I was here."

Flynae shakes her head, her throat closing, her heart racing. *I can't do this.*

The girl reaches out and touches her hand, capturing Flynae's attention. "Would you play a little for me? I love to listen when you play."

The Kaliah's stomach clenches. Her lip trembles. The human's adoration is so endearing. How could she say no?

Flynae stands and racks her brain for a tune to begin with as she walks to the piano. She sits down. Her fingers touch the ivory keys. One key after another begins to sing as her hands dance to create music.

46

E111 Influence (Flynae)

In spite of Kovad spooning her in their space every night as she falls asleep, Flynae continues to have nightmares over the next several days. Her words, "Don't touch me," plague her mind. She observes herself push him away over and over. When she rouses from one of these disturbing dreams, her stomach is in tight, painful knots.

Jasna sits with her every evening as she trains to transfer the slave mark. Flynae wakes up each morning with the human cuddling her in the closet.

The girl's death weighs heavy on the Kaliah's mind. No matter how she runs scenarios, Flynae can't find a way to save the human.

Every morning, Jasna leads her out to eat breakfast. The human piles her plate high with sweets and devours them but eats very little the rest of the day. She eyes Flynae like an overbearing mother, complete with raised eyebrows and occasional foot tapping, until the Kaliah chooses something to ingest besides alcohol. Each day, Flynae finds her more endearing than the one before.

The training ebbs and flows like a tide. Sometimes, the progress is astounding, but the setbacks are devastating. Every three steps forward are followed by two back, but Flynae has a difficult time celebrating the advancement. Kovad gently scolds her negativity and reminds her of her successes.

***

"Flynae. Wake up." Jasna shakes her.

Flynae starts awake. "What?"

She inhales and smells the human's mild alarm.

"The Emperor is here. We need to go out."

Flynae recalls the chime over the intercom she'd noticed but ignored moments ago. She'd only heard it once, the last time the Emperor visited the harem in person.

Her back is cold when the human jumps up. Flynae is loath to follow. Her blood boils with the memory of the lives the Emperor took.

Finally, she calmly walks out having composed herself. She won't let him win.

The rest of the women kneel in a circle around the fountain while he ogles one scantily clad body before moving on to the next.

Not wanting to create trouble, Flynae drops to her knees as well.

Seko stops in front of her. His odor changes from approval to several days old garbage.

She breathes heavily, disgusted with his hubris.

Suddenly, the two Kaliah guards rush her, grabbing her arms and pinning her against the nearby wall.

Seko presses his body against her and leers down at her. "You continue to encourage an air of defiance. No matter. In the end, I always win. Just look at your father."

Flynae refuses to allow her eyes to waver from his. With an inhale, she realizes that the room is filled with respect and adoration for her and disgust for the Emperor. No wonder he's threatened whenever he's around her. Even the two guards holding her in place smell more of duty than resolution.

"You're growing old." She swallows hard, resisting the lump in her throat that would silence her. "And afraid. Your power and influence are failing you like never before."

The Emperor's dark eyes begin burning red. Nothing else could have signaled she was close to the truth so clearly.

"You forget your place, child." Seko takes two steps back and turns to a third guard. "Strip her." He undresses from the waist down while the man obeys. "We'll see what they think of you when they discover you are nothing more than them, a toy to be used and discarded any time I want."

Unwilling to show weakness, Flynae breathes deeply and withstands the urge to flee into her mind and find Kovad. Lord Thyde is distracted and won't notice her if she doesn't panic. She needs a few more moments of defiance before she hides.

Her eyes don't blink when Seko roughly penetrates her.

Every other being in the room exudes revulsion.

"You're losing them. One by one. Their forced loyalty is slipping through your fingers," she says boldly.

Flynae breaks eye contact long enough to confirm her suspicion. The face of every soldier in the room is unknown to her. Seko needs to keep anyone exposed to her once away from her in the future. Without any conscious intention, she must be having an impact on them at a deep enough level that the Emperor is concerned about their further fealty when it entails her.

Seko slaps her.

"You think you have that influence?" His eyes narrow to slivers as an evil smile curls the corners of his lips. "Let's observe how revered you are as they watch you take it up your ass."

He breaks away from her and motions for the guards to bring her into the banquet room. At his sign, one of them pulls a tablecloth and everything on it to the floor.

Flynae releases a small gasp when her pelvic bone connects with the cold wood as the men holding her arms pull her torso down to the table. The last thing she's aware of before retreating inwardly is her feet dangling in the air, unable to touch the floor.

She turns her attention to Lord Thyde and begins running to his presence. *Kovad!*

47

E112 Just a Scratch (Kovad)

For the last twenty years, Lord Thyde trained with Anduryn most mornings. He's fully aware that the being who disguises himself as a human is a Kaliah and a spy for the Emperor.

They're engaged in lifesword sparring when Kovad hears Flynae scream his name. Her sudden call causes him to turn his attention and his head. He fails to bring his weapon up to block, and Anduryn's lifesword connects with his upper arm creating a shallow gash that begins bleeding.

Flynae's eyes widen with horror as she realizes she's at fault for the injury, but she doesn't slow her sprint toward him.

"Go," Kovad sternly commands the Kaliah in the room with him before turning his full focus to Flynae. He knows something horrible is happening. She never rushes to him but waits for him to approach her.

What is it, baby? He grips her and turns away from whatever nightmare she's fleeing.

You're bleeding. She reaches up to touch his arm and despairs when she can't do anything about the physical wound from a distance.

To appease her, he glances at the cut. Blood slowly seeps out.

Just a scratch. Nothing of any consequence.

He notices when her attention slips to her feet swaying slightly in the air. She constricts in his arms as her body experiences a searing, tearing pain. She breaks down into tears.

Kovad realizes he hasn't created a distraction for her. He physically sits down against a wall and brings to mind their favorite meadow.

Shut the rest out and be here with me, baby.

Flynae nestles as close as she can to his presence. *How many hours until Seko's speech?*

Kovad glances down at his wrist comm. *Six hours.*

Doubt floods her. Seko couldn't have chosen a worse morning to assault her. *What if I'm not recovered by the afternoon? We might need to delay.*

No. His tone is more forceful than he intends. *I'm not waiting another day knowing you're dying in that hell.* He takes a breath to calm his flaring temper. *I hold every confidence that you're capable of doing this today. And if you aren't then I'll be fighting by your side.*

What's with these sudden suicidal tendencies, Lord Thyde?

He wonders if her random use of his title in their space is a ploy to make him consider the things in his life beyond her. *You're more important to me than anything. I can't stand idly by while the Emperor continues to abuse and torment you.*

Her throat tightens with emotion. *I need you alive.* She clutches his hand. *You can't leave me yet.*

Then we can't fail today.

Alright. She strengthens her resolve. *We won't.*

Her body jerks as the Emperor finishes and throws her to

the floor. When part of her attention drifts back to controlling her person, Kovad sees the entire morning in her memory. He breathes through a flash of rage and disgust.

I'm so sorry, baby, he whispers.

"Clean her up and make sure she's ready to escort me in two hours." Seko motions for his guards to follow and glides from the room.

A sea of women with tear-streaked faces descend to help her, but Flynae holds up a hand to halt them. Having their painful emotions this close is enough. She doesn't need them all touching her.

Jasna pushes through the crowd and helps Flynae to her feet. "Let's get you washed."

Don't leave me, she begs, holding tight to Kovad's mental presence.

I'm not going anywhere.

Flynae curls into a ball in the bathtub, fighting nausea and debilitating cramps in her lower torso.

Jasna gently washes her with jasmine vanilla bath oils and salts.

Kovad focuses on comforting her as a means to ignore the hands on her skin.

48

E113 Belong (Kovad)

Lord Thyde stands behind Seko in a line with the other Lords while the Emperor delivers his bullshit to a crowd of wealthy elites. The words fade into a background drone as he stares past the people to where she sits on a bench waiting. Two human guards stand directly behind her.

She doesn't take her eyes off him. Her keen vision relishes the view.

When she inhales, he tastes the life and cleanness in the air, a stark contrast to the recycled air on the battleships. Her ears tune out the Emperor's voice, choosing to listen to some nearby birds chirping and whistling instead.

When the breeze blows in her direction, he notices she picks out his scent from among all the others and a soft smile plays with the corners of her mouth.

He watches her frequently shift her position as she's unable to find a way to sit that isn't agony. His hands clench and relax over and over as they yearn to grip her side and provide her with a painful pleasure that makes all other discomforts disappear.

Finally, Seko stops. After a round of applause, the Lords follow him from the platform and are dismissed until dinner in an hour.

Kovad focuses on keeping his pace to his normal speed while he walks from view to the airfield where the shuttles sit in rows. The unmarked shuttle where they'll meet is at the far end. He glances around making certain no one else is around as he approaches and enters it.

Once he's in place, she consumes his attention.

Flynae turns to the guards behind her. "I need to go to the bathroom."

"We are to keep you here until the Emperor signals otherwise."

Drawing on her ability to enchant and manipulate, Flynae pushes mentally as she stands up and pivots to look at them. "I'm going now."

The taller of the two gives in immediately. "Yes, ma'am."

Guard Two resists. "We are to remain here."

Flynae pulls from Kovad and influences them more forcefully. She grimaces when the guard's mental resolve begins crumbling. Finally, he breaks. The two soldiers follow her as she starts walking away at a barely controlled natural pace so as not to draw undue attention.

Guilt gnaws at her. How is she different from the Emperor if she's using identical tactics?

This is not the same, baby. You aren't trying to control their entire lives.

After confirming the park restroom is vacant, the guards wait outside while she goes in. Once the door swings shut, she implants the idea to them that she's still inside. When she comes out and walks between them, neither of them is aware of her.

Her heart pounds against her ribcage as she proceeds calmly to the airfield. A quick energy scan reveals the area is mostly deserted. She hones in on Lord Thyde's presence and begins running.

He exits the shuttle and watches for her, his body full of nervous tension. Finally, she appears, sprinting towards him, her hair and skirt flowing behind her.

Kovad kneels when she gets close, and Flynae barely slows. She crashes into him with a force that almost knocks him over backward. Her arms fall around his neck while her head and shoulders rest against his.

"Kovad," she whispers aloud for the first time.

"Hi, baby," he breathes on her neck. One hand finds her waist and squeezes.

She moans lightly.

For a moment, Lord Thyde is completely at peace. He's spent his entire life searching for something to bring him fulfillment. His constant drive to succeed propelled him through the military ranks. When he became a Lord, a brief instant of celebration turned to melancholy as he realized there was nothing else to strive for, no place higher to climb.

With his arms around her now, he experiences the greatest calm he's ever known. She is where he belongs. Nothing matters except her. He would be content to exist with her for eternity.

Tranquil bliss turns to fury as he notices her violently trembling. Her muscles ache with the quaking she can't stop.

"No," she whines. "Go back to the first smell."

He can't help but smile at the sound of her playful complaint. "Whatever you want, baby," he replies, turning his thoughts back to desires of holding her for the rest of his life.

"Mmm." Flynae inhales deeply.

Her fingertips trace the back of his neck sending shivers down his spine. She lightly scratches into his hairline with her claws before her hand runs over his shoulder and down his arm to find the wound hidden beneath clothes and bandages.

His skin tingles under her palm. A gentle warmth flows as the cut knits and heals like nothing happened.

"You should be saving your strength," he whispers.

"Yes. But you'll need yours, too."

He scoops her up and carries her inside.

49

E114 Ready (Kovad)

Lord Thyde sits down and cradles her, savoring the delicate substance of her in his arms. For a few seconds, her shaking calms as she relaxes against him.

He presses his cheek to her head. His hands grip and squeeze her. He turns and inhales her hair, wishing he could smell her the way she does him.

Flynae takes a breath, focusing on herself for a moment instead of him. Kovad experiences her aroma and holds her even tighter. She's the sweetest, most delicious thing he's ever encountered, and he can't get enough.

His body lights up, tingling and aching for more of her. All he wants is to smother her with kisses.

The perfect, bare skin of her shoulder catches his eye. His lips purse firmly as he struggles with his resolve to remain appropriate in the whirlwind of how intensely he desires her.

Flynae's hand presses against his chest, pushing him away, as she retakes her feet.

"We don't have time," she whispers.

Reluctantly, he nods his acknowledgment and stands next to her.

She makes a small energy shield around him, stopping his aura from being detected outside the shuttle.

As he looks down at her, he can't help but think about how small and fragile she appears. Her body visibly quivers under the weight of the task before them.

Flynae opens her mouth to speak, but her words come out too quietly for human ears to hear. She takes a couple shallow breaths.

"Deep breaths, Flynae," he says softly, reaching out to comfort her.

Startled by the movement, she shrieks and flinches. Her hands fly up to cover her face. *I'm sorry.* She struggles to get her breathing under control.

"Baby. Don't apologize. It's okay."

Kovad realizes he didn't notice how close to falling apart she is. Her psyche is at the edge of a cliff with her toes hanging off the ledge. The slightest breeze could send her over.

She lowers her hands. Her eyes remain down, unable to meet his. *Hold out your hand like you're holding a pen.*

He extends his left arm, his thumb and index finger touching while the other three fingers curl.

Flynae takes a step closer and cups her hands lightly around his. Energy swirls around and between them. Then he feels something solid between his fingers. The object elongates until he's gripping a dull gold feather pen.

Flynae takes a full inhale and lifts her gaze to his. "I, Flynae Let, by royal decree, grant you, Lord Kovad Thyde, permission to claim for your own the slave, Flynae Let."

His left hand tingles. He glances down to see the pen glowing and sparkling brilliantly.

He returns to her wide, unblinking eyes, marveling at the trust she's putting in him. How had he ever done enough to earn it?

"Ready?" she whispers.

He watches her rub her sweaty palms on the skirt of her dress.

"Ready." He swallows with difficulty, finding a sudden lump in his throat. "What do I do?"

Flynae turns around, dropping the spaghetti strap off her left shoulder and slipping her arm out of it.

"You should see your initials faintly overlaying Eksar's." She absentmindedly brings a hand to rest over her nervous, cramping stomach while she talks. "You just need to trace what you see. Be sure to press hard enough to break the skin."

The outline of the slave mark on her shoulders glows with a light similar to the pen. The letters KT are clearly visible above the EL.

"Umm," she continues as something else significant returns to her cognitive thought. "You'll have to hold me down." Her eyes land on the small table in the shuttle. "You can use your weight to pin me against that."

His jaw tightens in revulsion. He hadn't considered the need to restrain her for the process. The thought makes him ill.

Her soft fingers slip around his empty hand. "It's okay." She gently pulls him towards her.

Lord Thyde stands behind her and watches her lower her torso to the cold, grey metal table.

The pressure is painful on her already bruised pelvis. Her feet dangle, unable to reach the floor. He steps forward, and his legs brush up against hers.

Flynae screams and pushes against him. He gives in and

backs away. She practically flies to the corner and hides her face again. All the sensations from the morning's violations flood her present awareness.

Her knees weaken and threaten to buckle. But she forces herself to remain on her feet, knowing it's all over if she gives in and sinks to the floor.

Kovad wants to go to her and hold her. As his foot starts to lift, he sees her constrict and stops.

Baby.

Just a minute. Just a minute. Just a minute. Her thoughts come wildly fast, the words tumbling over one another.

He begins breathing loudly and slowly. Inhale for a count of four. Pause. Exhale for four. Pause. Repeat.

Her ears zone in on the sound, and she listens. Within a minute or so, her breath pattern matches his.

One of her hands reaches out for him. Trying not to rush, he moves forward and clasps it.

"Okay." She blinks to clear her vision and walks over to press her shoulders against his torso. "Be ready to start immediately. And once we begin, we can't stop."

He leans with her most of the way this time. His right arm rests across her upper back; his left hand poised above the mark. He's painfully aware of his crotch pressed against her butt and how she'd been demeaned in the same position hours before.

When he notices her attention returning to her hanging feet, unable to touch the floor, he presses the pen into her shoulder.

50

E115 The Slave Mark (Kovad)

Flynae's body bucks against him as she screams. The noise is shrill and painful to his ears while it hurts his soul on a deeper level. Tears fall from his face to her back which already glistens with a sheen of sweat.

Her strength surprises him as she involuntarily fights, and he leans most of his weight against her shoulder keeping her in place.

Her legs and feet kick violently, bruising his shins. One of her feet begins pressing against his leg, pushing him away. He widens his stance to maintain a close footing.

The resistance from the slave mark is shocking. He'd hoped to rush through the tracing and be done quickly. Now he understands why they'd needed to train for stamina. The tip of the pen refuses to move faster than a millimeter at a time.

Lord Thyde's vision blurs further as the sound of her agony overwhelms him. He'd inflicted pain on so many people in his military career: men, women, even children. He'd killed without regret. But he can't handle hurting her.

The stylus stops moving. He tries to force it, but it won't

budge.

He blinks to clear his eyes and sees he's heading off the track, but it won't let him. After a slight angle adjustment, he's able to continue.

At last, the first stroke of the K is complete.

He lifts his arm and wipes his face which is covered in sweat and tears.

Kovad. Her thought is weak and sounds far away.

What is it?

I need air.

Huh?

I can't breathe.

Finally comprehending, he removes his weight from her.

Flynae gasps.

Across her shoulder is the beginning of a bruise where his arm had been. He stares down at it in horror.

Kovad. Refocus. We have to hurry. Eksar's coming.

Okay, baby. His heart pounds furiously. He releases a resigned sigh and leans on her again.

When the quill punctures her skin, the noise she makes sounds more like a weak mewling kitten than a humanoid. Her body is too exhausted to be loud. He finds he doesn't have to put as much weight on her, which is comforting because then he doesn't have to worry about her passing out from lack of air.

Finally, the K is finished.

Lord Thyde lifts the pen and takes a breath. When another bead of sweat falls from his chin, he follows it down to find a pool on her back. Her dress is soaked.

His stomach tightens into a knot of revulsion at the defilement of her regal body. He doesn't dare hesitate further to retrieve a towel and presses the feather pen against her. The point refuses to puncture the mark.

"Flynae?" He gently shakes her with no response.

"Baby?" Kovad rolls her over.

She's unresponsive, her eyes closed.

They had talked and prepared for this. The shuttle's refrigerator was turned down to the lowest setting and stocked with several bottles of water. Kovad doesn't hesitate to grab one. When he holds it over her face, he pauses, hating himself for having to rouse her in this manner.

His eyes squeeze shut as he tilts the bottle and pours. The water splatters over her face.

He feels like he's falling through ice to frigid water below. Her voice calls his name before she shouts, "Don't touch me!"

A moment later, she begins choking and coughing. "What?"

Her eyes open but only barely. Her oval pupils reflect the overhead light.

"I'm sorry, baby. We have to hurry."

"Kovad?"

"I'm here, baby. I can't do this without you." He experiences the building pressure of a great furry racing towards them. They're both dead if she can't finish.

"Okay," she murmurs. "Roll me over."

She regathers her focus and combines their energies for the purpose.

He presses the tip of the pen into her flesh and holds it, waiting for the mark to give. Finally, the quill punctures her.

She releases a sob. He watches her body twitch in pain, but she doesn't have the strength to struggle.

"Stay with me, Flynae." Now that he knows what to expect and what he's doing, he can focus on her more. Keeping her awake is of utmost importance.

The first tall stroke of the T is finished.

With barely any forethought, he leans down and kisses her shoulder. "That's my girl. You've got this. I'm so proud of you. Just a moment more."

She nods her head slightly.

"This is it." He hovers over her and slits her skin a final time.

Time slows as he curses the snail's pace of the pen. Seconds pass like someone beating a gong in slow motion.

Then he reaches the end of the line. The mark burns a hot red before fading to look like a healed brand. The EL is gone, replaced by a KT.

A new connection to her forms in his mind, almost instantaneously. With dawning horror, he recognizes the power over her she's given him. Something akin to a lever resides in his energy field that will incapacitate her with a thought. He begins sweating anew, hoping that he can't accidentally trip it.

Eksar's energy rushes in and pulls up outside the shuttle. Both of them sense his arrival.

From somewhere, Kovad feels Flynae gathering energy into herself. She renews the shield around him, protecting her human, before she pushes herself to her feet.

The hairs on his arm stand on end in response to the electric field around her as she takes a couple of steps and positions her body between him and the door. Her hair and dress flow and swirl with a wind he can't detect. Light glints from her skin.

51

E116 Enough (Kovad)

Lord Thyde feels her vortex enveloping his energy completely, hiding it within.

Eksar paces outside, his aura one of equal rage, surprise, and fear.

Flynae's full focus is pushing Eksar away, making the power flowing around her insurmountable enough that the older Kaliah flees. She doesn't want to face and fight him. Not after all the effort she and Kovad expended.

Lord Thyde hears a pounding heartbeat and realizes she's listening to the one immediately outside. Gradually, the thumping grows quieter. Eksar is moving away.

Her attention shifts from the sound to her uncle's energy as he retreats. Finally, he is far enough away, and she relaxes.

Kovad observes her hair and skirt cease their swirling. For a moment, his head is light like he's about to pass out. Then he realizes he's experiencing her faint in time to spring forward and down to his knees to catch her before she crashes to the floor.

"I've got you, baby," he whispers, holding her close. He

strokes her hair. "You did so well."

"You have to go."

Her words are barely audible. He perceives them in his mind more than with his ears.

Lord Thyde glances around and realizes they'd neglected to plan a place for her to lay.

"On the floor. Just set me down and go."

"Corporal West." Kovad's voice shifts from the gentle tone he uses with her to his strong, stern public one.

A soldier, dressed in military fatigues used by the Emperor's footmen, appears from the cockpit. Beneath his short brown hair, his eyes are bright red and swollen, his face stained with tears.

"My lord." West slightly chokes as he speaks.

"Take her to The Apparition and wait for me there."

"Yes, my lord." The soldier nods.

"Have blankets and pillows brought for her and see that she is kept warm. Do *not* touch her without her permission. Do not leave her alone. Obey her words as if they were mine." He pauses for a quick exhale as he considers what he missed. "And if anything happens to her, you'd better be dead."

"Yes, my lord."

With great reluctance, Kovad lays Flynae on the cold metal floor. He takes her hand and presses her fingers to his lips.

Go. I love you. The last sentence flows out naturally and without apology. She would rather say them to him than goodbye.

Flynae, I– His thought cuts off. Those last two words gnaw at him, wanting to be let out to reassure her, but he holds them back.

Her hand squeezes his. *It's okay. I can smell you. That's*

enough.

He kisses her fingers again, gently sets her arm down, and strides from the shuttle before he finds another reason to delay and remain with her.

The vehicle's engine fires to life.

Lord Thyde stands a safe distance away and watches as it lifts and disappears into the sky. Only once it vanishes from sight, does he turn and move towards the one he arrived in.

As he walks, he's bothered by the last phrase she said. *That's enough. No, it's not enough. She's settling, and she shouldn't ever settle for anything, especially with me. I should be giving her more. Everything.*

But the two words he can't say hold back a whole domino of actions he needs to refrain from. If he tells her he loves her, then why wouldn't it also be permissible and a reasonable next step to kiss her neck?

The curve of her perfect marble skin appears in his thoughts.

And if she allowed him to do that, then why not her lips next?

The kissing would lead to bruising her higher on her rib cage where his thumb could brush the slightest swell of her breast. And if those actions weren't already too much, he craves taking her to his bed and sleeping with her body pressed against his all night long.

The battle between wanting to do more than *enough* and stay in control continues to wage within him, elevating his heart rate and tightening his chest.

Kovad, please calm down. She's worried his energy won't be neutral by the time he rejoins the Emperor. Flynae doesn't want Seko or Eksar to suspect anything about Lord Thyde concerning her disappearance, though that isn't entirely possible.

Mostly to appease her, he starts taking deep full breaths and pushes the other thoughts from his mind. Within moments, his well-practiced body is void of all emotional influences.

By the time he reaches his shuttle, he has about twenty minutes before he'll be missed. With time to spare, he showers and changes to a fresh outfit identical to what he was wearing.

When he arrives at the banquet hall, The Emperor and Eksar stand outside talking in hushed voices. Seko's eyes darken and narrow when he notices Kovad.

"Lord Thyde. You wouldn't have anything to do with this, would you?"

Maintaining a casual composure, he replies, "I wouldn't know unless you explain what you are referring to."

Eksar inhales a hissing breath.

Seko holds up his hand, stopping the Kaliah from saying anything. "The mysterious disappearance of my date for this evening."

"Maybe you should ask those you assigned to guard her."

The Emperor glides to Kovad and stands close; his fingertips touch the human's chest like someone flirting with a lover. He looks up into Lord Thyde's eyes.

"If I find out you were involved with her vanishing, then I will give you a choice. You may either take her in front of 50 of my officers. Or. You can watch those same officers take her one after the other."

Lord Thyde swallows hard, unable to keep himself from reacting.

"Do I make myself clear, my Lord?"

"Yes, my liege."

"Good. Now, let's go to dinner." Seko turns and begins walking to the entrance. He pauses next to Eksar. "Find her. Now."

With a tight face, Eksar glares at Kovad before retreating to do his master's bidding.

Lord Thyde follows the Emperor inside.

52

E117 Zeresh (Kovad)

Time taunts him as it slides along at a snail's pace. By the time the amuse is served, Flynae is asleep. Lord Thyde wishes she'd been unconscious for the brief exchange with the Emperor. Those were words she didn't need to worry herself about.

He can't help but replay the sound of her singing as the evening's entertainment pales in comparison to her performance a few weeks back. Once again, he feels his arms around her as they danced the tango together.

One day, he promises himself, *I'll be able to dance with her as often as she desires.*

The vision they'd shared while she made the lifesword teases him. In a possible future reality, she belongs to only him. How do they arrive there? Are they on the correct path? One single misstep could demolish the dream forever.

He replays the scene, as well as his flawed human memory can, wanting a view that will show him the slave mark on her shoulder. Whose initials reside on her shoulder in that time to come?

As much as he tries, he doesn't recall seeing the mark. Flynae was napping on her back when he'd gone to her. And when he'd slid her dress from her, he'd viewed her entire front.

Suddenly, his pants are uncomfortably tight, and he shifts in his seat.

The Emperor turns and tilts his head slightly to glance at Kovad out of the corner of his eye.

Lord Thyde banishes the thoughts of her naked body and returns his attention to the evening's entertainment so that it can bore him. Within minutes, he's thinking about Flynae again. Was she still on the cold floor? Had she allowed Corporal West to move her from it?

She should be safe aboard The Apparition. The warship was the headquarters for all his spy vehicles. As far as he knew, the Emperor was not aware of its existence.

Kovad's mindful of the Emperor's attention on him and knows he's not being as neutral as he needs to be. Daydreaming about Flynae constantly isn't helping. He turns his focus to listening to the musicians. If she was awake, she would enjoy their music.

And there I go thinking about her again.

Each second is agony knowing he could walk outside, take his shuttle, and be with her. But that would put them both in jeopardy.

Seko's threat weighs heavy on his mind. The only peace Kovad brings to himself concerning it is the hope that the Emperor needs her more than he wants to torment her. Lord Thyde can't bring himself to imagine what he would do if the nightmare scenario became reality.

When dinner is over, the evening is far from finished. The Emperor planned an after party especially to induct Lord

Zeresh. Lord Thyde prays that Flynae remains asleep during it.

The new Lord's presence is despicable to Kovad. Zeresh exudes an evil similar to the Emperor. The man is cruel to anyone he thinks of as a lesser.

Lord Thyde settles in his seat in Seko's playroom aboard The Dominion and begins to tune everything around him out. Not wanting to wake her up, he does a gentle check to be certain Flynae is still asleep. He plans on ignoring as much of the noise and visuals as he can, but he'll be more relaxed if he knows he doesn't have to be super vigilant about her being aware of what is happening.

The room lights dim. The stage lights turn on. Kovad averts his gaze to the same familiar spot on the floor.

The music starts, and the show begins.

Lord Thyde focuses on his breathing and reaches a nearly meditative state. He's unsure how much time has passed when a female voice he recognizes cuts through his light trance.

When he looks up, his heart rate surges; and he blinks several times to verify what he thinks he sees.

Jasna walks forward and kneels before the Emperor. "My liege."

Seko turns to the newest member of his exclusive club. "Lord Zeresh. Your prize for the evening."

Zeresh stands over the small girl and eagerly rubs his hands together.

Kovad's skin crawls with disgust. As if in response, Seko's mouth widens in a gleeful leer.

Lord Thyde returns his attention to his breath, blocking out as much of what occurs next, hoping to save Flynae from witnessing what happens.

When they're finally dismissed, he can't stop himself from

looking at the carnage and seeing the battered, bloodied body of Flynae's blonde friend.

His throat is tight as he hurries to his shuttle and pilots to The Destroyer. Wanting to be sure he isn't being followed, he takes one of his unmarked shuttles and flies to the nearest planet. He exchanges that vehicle for a third. Then he finally travels to The Apparition.

53

E118 Everything I Want (Kovad)

As soon as he lands in the hanger bay, Lord Thyde rushes from his shuttle to the one where she lays. When her heart rate increases at the sound of his hurrying steps, he forces himself to slow.

The ramp begins to open and lower. Kovad is aware of Corporal West moving from sitting to standing, a severe breach of protocol. His temper flares until she whispers, *I asked him to.*

Why?

Actually, he resisted until I realized I needed to tell him. He was very conflicted about complying with a request.

That's fine. But why?

I felt weird with him standing over me. Did I do something wrong?

Never. You can't do anything wrong, baby.

Finally, the entrance is open enough for him to jump and walk inside.

Corporal West stiffens and stands at rigid attention.

"At ease, soldier," Lord Thyde says before kneeling next to

her.

Flynae is hidden under a mountain of comforters except for strands of her brilliant scarlet hair. She's turned away from the doorway, facing the opposite direction he'd left her in. She looks up at him as he leans over her.

"Kovad," she breathes. Her cheeks glow as she stares at him, unwilling to even blink. A playful grin forms on her face.

"Hi, baby." He smiles, unable to stop himself at the sight of her face, and tucks back some of the blankets to touch the skin of her upper arm. He's relieved to find her body warm since that was a constant concern all evening.

Underneath her are several more layers of covers. She must have allowed Corporal West to roll her onto them.

"May I lift you? We're going back to The Destroyer. The Emperor might suspect something, but he didn't have me followed."

She nods while her body tightens involuntarily, bracing for the inevitable pain.

Kovad uncovers her and pulls her into his arms. Because of her current fatigue, he supports and cradles her head.

She exhales a small cry that cuts and twists his emotions like a knife. From the corner near the entrance, the other human sniffs.

Lord Thyde turns and glares at the subordinate, ready to give a tongue-lashing.

Kovad. Her soft thought stops him and returns his attention to her. *Your eyes are watering too.*

When he looks down, his vision of her is obscured and swimming. She's right. He sighs and releases his judgment of West.

Her body is almost weightless as he grips her tightly and

stands up. He turns to the waiting soldier.

"Scrap the vehicle for a new one and return to your post on The Dominion. Keep me apprised of the Emperor's movements."

"Yes, my lord." Corporal West's eyes drop with another lapse in protocol.

Lord Thyde realizes the man's returning Flynae's gaze and wonders who would be able to resist looking into her eyes.

"Thank you, Davyn," she says, requiring a lot of effort to make her voice loud enough.

"My pleasure, my lady." He lowers his head and closes his eyes momentarily in deference before resuming a pose of perfect attention.

"Dismissed," Kovad says, recognizing with a touch of pride that he'd chosen the ideal soldier to guard her until he could return.

Davyn West nods once and marches from the shuttle.

Lord Thyde carries Flynae to a new vehicle and buckles her into the copilot seat before sitting in the pilot's chair.

"I'm not sure I have the requisite faculties to sit here," she says, smiling.

"I wasn't about to let you out of my sight again tonight."

They pass the flight in silence. He watches the stars through her eyes, which can slow down and observe one in detail at lightspeed.

When they arrive at The Destroyer, he carries her to the couch in her quarters and sits down with her in his arms.

"What will you eat?" he asks softly, knowing she hasn't ingested anything all day. Her first moment of the day was consumed with the announcement of the Emperor's presence.

Her mind goes blank. She searches without finding an

answer.

Kovad tries to think about what he's seen her consume but finds she eats so little. "Soup? Salmon? Eggs?"

"I'll try some soup."

He knows she doesn't want it. He observes her body rejecting every option she thinks of. Still, he speaks in his comm ordering butternut squash soup, knowing she'd eaten that on Halaa.

She rests against him, enjoying the warmth of his body, the beating of his heart so close to her ear, and his protective smell.

When the food arrives, he holds the bowl when her inclination is to sip from it rather than bother with a spoon. Her hands shake beneath his.

Gradually, his stomach hurts and churns. His throat constricts.

She coughs, choking slightly.

Kovad realizes she's eating only to please him; her body's revolting against the sustenance. He sets the container aside.

"Baby." He tightens his arms around her with desperation. Tears fill his eyes. "What can I get you? Wine? Anything?"

Her gentle weight presses into him. With a great effort, she reaches her hand up and strokes the back of his neck. "I have everything I want."

He strengthens his grasp on her, his elbows on her shoulders, his hands on her head, clutching her tightly. "So do I, baby." He leans and touches his lips to her head as tears pour down his cheeks.

54

E119 I Want You (Kovad)

Kovad leans back against the couch and closes his eyes. Flynae relaxes against him.

"You called me 'your girl'," she says softly.

"I did. Aren't you?"

She takes a few deep inhales, savoring his scent. Her fingers caress his skin.

His heart pounds in anticipation, needing to hear her say it. His hand slides down to tighten over her side as if to convey he'll give her everything she desires from him.

"I am."

He squeezes her ever tighter until she moans. "You don't miss anything, do you?"

"I try not to. Especially when it comes to you." She yawns and tries to stifle the sound.

Kovad pulls the blanket off the back of the couch and drapes the soft fabric over her. Then he de-stresses with a brief mental rundown of his day. The ritual is similar to meditation before sleep. Recapping everything important prevents the events from impacting his rest. The images pass like a quick blur until he's nearly unconscious.

Flynae's words pull him awake. "You saw Jasna." Her observation morphs into horror when she sees the girl's end in his memories. "No."

Adrenaline overrides fatigue as she sits up and throws her arms around his neck. Devastation at her friend's death becomes despair at the thought of his.

"You can't leave me. I won't let you." She lowers her head to his shoulder and begins sobbing.

A great rush of emotions threatens to overwhelm him. He notices the whip held by his hand land against her back. A strip of red blooms and oozes on her marble skin. He stares as her body lurches forward, her feet losing their footing and sliding back to reclaim balance.

You are nothing more than them, a toy to be used and discarded any time I want. The Emperor's words replay in her mind. *Let's see how revered you are as they watch you take it up the ass.*

Flynae twists and jerks as the insults take hold and dig into her psyche.

My daughter does not sleep with trash. Eksar's voice joins Seko's.

Please don't ask for something that would make me despise myself. Kovad hears his plea and tone twisted in her memory.

She is garbage.

The words repeat.

Toy.

Discarded.

Trash.

Despise.

She's tainted.

Soiled.

Ruined.

Why would anyone want her after what Seko and Eksar did to her?

She writhes in anguish.

Flynae.

She doesn't acknowledge him.

Baby, he pleads.

"My love," he whispers aloud.

He grabs the back of her head, his fingers slipping through her hair to pull her close. *I want you. I want all of you. Don't listen to anything they say about you. None of it is true.*

She's still and quiet, tears no longer flowing. Her mind is empty. The only reason he knows she heard him is the way she's pressing against him.

Suddenly, her body starts trembling, slightly at first but increasing in intensity.

"Did I say something wrong?"

She shakes her head but otherwise doesn't respond.

He sits silently, waiting for any signal from her. She doesn't move, doesn't think a single word.

"You should sleep, baby. You're exhausted." His fatigue starts to creep back, but he won't give in until she is safely sleeping.

Flynae nods. Her hand slips down to his arm and holds on like she's afraid he'll disappear if she doesn't. Her eyes close, but her body continues to painfully shake, taking her breath away.

Kovad breathes slowly and deeply for her.

After a few minutes of focusing on him, she eases into unconsciousness. Only then does he shut his eyes.

At first, sleep is peaceful and dreamless. Gradually, a soft noise builds.

"Shhh. Shhh." The ice whispers beneath a skate blade. "Shhh."

The sound is calming and welcome.

Until the ice cracks. The shushing stops as he falls into the freezing water with a splash. Except he isn't in the water. He's watching the dream from her eyes. And she's looking up at his outstretched hand.

Flynae leaps for him and misses. Her body shivers and grows numb. She reaches again and connects with him this time.

Kovad pulls her out and holds her close. She relaxes in his arms for a moment before she screams, "Don't touch me," and shoves him away.

"Stop it! Stop it!" she yells in a furious rage. "I'm not doing this anymore."

With alarm, he watches warrior Flynae throw the child off a great cliff.

Lord Thyde starts awake. Flynae's hand is on his chest, pushing herself up and off his lap. He opens his eyes in time to see her crash to the floor.

She scampers on her hands and knees to a corner where she curls up tightly, burying her face against her legs.

"What did you do?" The last image he witnessed feels of great significance. He's still shaking off sleep and his body is heavy with fatigue as he stands and takes a couple steps toward her.

She constricts, flinching away from him, her body visibly quaking.

Kovad drops to his knees. "Baby."

Don't call me that.

His lips part slightly in surprise. "Why?" *You don't mean*

that.

I can't. I can't. I can't.

55

E120 Can't (Kovad)

"Can't what?" Lord Thyde stares across the room at her small, trembling form. Her response confuses him. He replays the early morning hours before they fell asleep.

A glance at his wrist comm reveals they only slept for an hour and a half. Exhaustion explains part of her actions but not nearly enough of them.

Flynae hadn't spoken again after he'd called her, "My love." Were those words to blame for her distress? Apparently, they hadn't helped the situation.

"Flynae," he says softly, reaching out a hand and inching towards her.

She shrieks and constricts further. The next moment, she jumps up, hugs the wall, and runs for the door. The short sleep was not sufficient for her to regain control of herself, and she falls again.

Kovad experiences the pain in her knee and chin from the impact.

Flynae retakes her feet and flees through her bedroom and

into the bathroom. She turns off the light and huddles in the corner of the cold tile floor of the shower.

Lord Thyde follows slowly, overly aware of the sound of his footfalls. He leans his head and hand against the closed door separating him from her.

Would you please talk to me? What can I do? He focuses on his breathing as his heart races and his temperature rises. He's always preferred to be angry rather than hurt and helpless, and his body is defaulting to rage now. The intense emotional pain at her distance threatens to overwhelm and destroy all self-control.

I can't. I can't. Her mental voice is weak and distant.

His fist tightens. Why isn't she talking to him? He grits his teeth and breathes through the urge to hit something. She's already broken. He doesn't need to add anything else to the mix.

Kovad turns around and slides his back down the door until he's sitting on the floor. He searches for her in her mind, but her part of their shared space is dark and cold.

Where are you, baby?

She releases a sob. *Please don't. You can't. I can't.*

Her stomach clenches and twists painfully.

Okay. I won't. But I'm begging you to talk to me.

He's aware of her rolling to her side and her sobs renewing.

I can't.

He leaps to his feet with a loud exhale, unable to continue listening to those two words. Hearing her say them over and over will drive him insane. He needs to move, to do something. Anything.

But he can't leave her hiding in the dark alone.

This isn't the way today was supposed to go. They should

still be sleeping to wake up several hours from now, rested and refreshed.

Kovad had planned to propose a picnic on the floor. She'd been relaxed and confident the last time they'd eaten together like that. He remembers her unpacking the different sushi containers, curious and delighted at the vast array he'd ordered. He was going to relax and have a mimosa with her.

As they ate, they would talk about next steps. He wants to know about the rush of energy and the vortex Flynae created. Does she know what she did? Could she replicate it?

Lord Thyde is aware that while he'd contributed to it slightly, most of the power had come from outside him and possibly even her. Seko and Eksar won't stand a chance if she's cognizant of how to do it again.

He shivers and realizes she's cold.

May I bring you a blanket?

No.

At first, the single-word response wounds him, but he turns it to irritation to avoid the pain. Why won't she let him help her? Every time he reaches out to her mentally, all he finds is darkness.

Is she trapped or hiding?

Kovad sits on the edge of the bed and dives into the nothing in her mind. The space is cold and sucks the warmth from his body.

The image of Flynae's warrior ego tossing the child returns to his recollection. Was that real or a dream? Did she do something that drastic? If yes, then he needs to find the child, the fragile delicate part she keeps trying to lock away or destroy.

From somewhere in the pitch black, he hears her quietly

crying. The noise comes from all directions giving him no idea which way to go first. Moving slowly, he decides on a trajectory and holds to it for several minutes. The volume of the weeping doesn't change. He's not getting closer.

Where are you? he asks.

Accompanying the blackness is heavy despair. Before all this, he remembers the awful statements she replayed in her head. The evil lies about her started the meltdown.

No. This catastrophe was long overdue. She held on for longer than most could. If she was going to break, this was the safest place.

Flynae, he calls out into the black nothing knowing she hears him on some level. *I want you.* Now is not the other time to repeat the word he resisted for so long.

You're incredible. You're so strong. And amazing. And beautiful. Take as long as you need. I'm here. I'm not going anywhere. As soon as you're ready, I'll come get you.

After an exhale, he adds, *I want you.*

The distance grows overwhelming as he thinks about giving her more space. He aches to hold and comfort her. *Please. Come back to me. Whenever you're ready.*

56

E121 Losing Her (Kovad)

Lord Thyde sniffs as his eyes tear up.

Unable to sit and be tormented by how close she is, he stands and strides from her apartment to his. What he needs if he's going to let her be is movement.

After changing into a sleeveless t-shirt and joggers, he hits the running track and pounds out 5 miles in thirty minutes.

While he exercises, he allows himself to come to terms with Flynae's need for distance.

The mindlink was renewed barely a month ago. She'd spent half that time alone in a dark closet. Socializing was dangerous as several women who were kind to her were dead now.

Her trauma response is normal, and he will respect it.

He can give her space and time to heal.

I'm here when you need me. Or want me. Take as long as you require.

She's quiet and unresponsive.

But let me bring you blankets. Or get them yourself, he thinks more to himself than her with a sigh. *And eat something.*

He groans and picks up his pace slightly, berating himself

for trying to impose his desires for her on her.

I want you to be comfortable, ba-. Kovad stops before he completes the word she doesn't want to hear from him.

Why!? he laments. For the past month, he couldn't think about Flynae without calling her baby. She's his girl. His love. Not addressing her with terms of endearment is agony.

However, the situation is fitting for him to suffer with her. The distance wouldn't be torment if he didn't care for her so deeply. If she's in pain, he should be hurting, too.

Without her, the sensation would be foreign. The only anguish he's endured in the last decade revolves around her. She's consumed and taken over his emotions. They all belong to her, and he doesn't know what to do with himself with her so far away.

When he finishes his run, he spends another thirty minutes lifting weights, pushing himself to fatigue trying to keep his thoughts from being wholly monopolized by her to no avail.

Rather than fighting the distraction that is Flynae, Lord Thyde lets his regular routine take over and autopilot him for a few hours.

After the workout, he showers and dresses. Food is next. Discipline causes him to ingest most of his normal breakfast, but his body or hers takes issue with the idea, making the process unpleasant.

Kovad sits at his desk and prepares a report to send to the Emperor. Keeping up appearances of normality will lessen suspicion concerning her possible presence on his ship.

Minutes crawl by like hours. Every time he scrolls or switches to something new, he glances at the time and checks in with her.

I'm here, Flynae. If nothing else registers in her awareness, he wants her to understand he'll come running to her without hesitation.

She doesn't move. Her status barely changes through the course of the day. She's cold. Hungry. Thirsty. Exhausted.

Occasionally, she closes her eyes and dozes. Without exception, the result is unchanging. The nightmare starts. The ice cracks. She falls into the frigid water. Kovad pulls her out. She wants him to hold her. She needs him to hold her. But she shoves him away with the same scream. And Flynae awakes with a start twenty to thirty minutes after she fell asleep.

Lord Thyde started his workday early and ends it early, his body rebelling and fatigued from lack of sleep. After a light dinner, he changes into a t-shirt and cotton pants and strides to her bedroom.

He doesn't want her to feel trapped, but he recognizes that trying to rest thirty feet away from her will be useless. He lays down on his back and sets the intention to sleep lightly and listen for her.

As he drifts off, he visualizes his desire for her to come out and curl up next to him.

***

Lord Thyde's internal alarm wakes him at his usual time to rise. When he turns his head and discerns the bathroom door is open, he knows she's gone. Not just absent from the nearby quarters but off The Destroyer completely.

Wherever Flynae is, she's sleeping or otherwise unconscious because her mind is perfectly blank.

Unwilling to trust his senses, he gets up and visually checks the shower. Upon going back to the bedroom, he finds the garment she was wearing the day before in the trash receptacle near the desk. He experiences the slightest joy in knowing she's dressed in something he purchased for her.

As he enters the sitting room, he notices two slips of paper on the piano. In flowing script resembling elegant calligraphy are two short sentences, "I'm so sorry. I love you."

The words sting though he doesn't fault her for her actions. He's delusional to believe she would be safe aboard his ship for long, but he desired to discuss and carry out a strategy with her.

The weight of her absence continues to build, and he sits down hard on the bench.

Several minutes pass before he commands himself to look at the other message. A corner of it is tucked under her lifesword. He's surprised she left her weapon behind.

"I didn't have the heart to separate the pair," the second note reads.

Kovad places his elbows on the closed piano lid and lowers his head to his hands. "The lifeswords only belong together because we belong together, baby."

About the Author

Hi!

I want everyone to know that I'm a sucker for lions, and I got to hold one on a vacation to Mexico.

I'm an author of all things dark and disturbing including horror, fantasy, and snippets of sci-fi. I started writing stories when I was ten years old. Some of my favorite stories at that age were The Hobbit and The Chronicles of Narnia.

After watching too many horror movies at a young age, I've only been able to sleep with my feet uncovered at night for a few years now.

I live with my husband Daniel, my cat Juno, our dogs Zelda and Ajax, the two goats Milo and Jasper, Simba the horse, and three unnamed chickens who are too old now to lay eggs and just cost us money.

My favorite hobbies are reading, writing, researching, singing, and listening to music. I believe that my writing is most influenced by J.R.R. Tolkien, Stephen King, and George

R.R. Martin.

You can connect with me on:

- https://linktr.ee/tirzahmmhawkins
- https://www.facebook.com/groups/tirzahmmhawkins

Also by Tirzah M.M. Hawkins

The Party is on Ream!!

If you've ever wanted to hang out and chat with an author about their stories, then you definitely need to join my Ream subscription. Why is it so great? I'm glad you asked.

Ream is where I host my private community for my fans. Feel free to follow me and just consume the free stuff which includes reviews of the books I read and certain free stories.

Or dive on in and sign up for a book box-level subscription. Every quarter, I send out a book box filled with signed books, fun items that I picked out or had made for you, and an item that I made or painted. That last thing used to be a paint pour, but I'm branching out into resin and other fun things.

You and I can dive deeper into my stories on Ream. Readers can leave comments on individual paragraphs as they read. I'll read those and respond when I have something to say back.

Want to dip your toe in? I made a custom code for you. ONEFREE

Enter that code when you sign up to get your first month as a Citizen or Courtier in my Ream realm for free. How does it get better than that?

I don't know, but it will. Especially if we keep asking.

I hope to see you on Ream. Find the link for it here: TirzahMMHawkins.com.

If you aren't interested in my subscription, then you can still find the links to everything that I've written and published at TirzahMMHawkins.com. That's the hub to find everything that I would like you to find.

9 798224 995257

Printed by Libri Plureos GmbH in Hamburg,
Germany